"So your boyfriend got you to steal my formula!"

Kane's face was ashen beneath its tan. "You're the only one with a master key to all the rooms in this hotel, and you knew he wanted to cut me out of that contract. So you sneaked into my suite and stole my specifications— and guess who presented them to the Japanese this morning, with a little help from Miss Kingston!"

"You're mad," Sharon cut in icily. "I wasn't anywhere near your suite last night, and unless you retract your accusations I'll be forced to ask for legal advice!"

Then she remembered Tassy, the beautiful Thai girl she'd seen coming from Kane's room, and anguish and jealousy swamped her. Not only were they lovers, but Tassy was a thief, as well....

Books by Roberta Leigh

LOVE MATCH

HARLEQUIN PRESENTS

HARLEQUIN ROMANCE

These books may be available at your local bookseller.

Don't miss any of our special offers. Write to us at the following address for information on our newest releases.

Harlequin Reader Service
P.O. Box 52040, Phoenix, AZ   85072-2040
Canadian address: P.O. Box 2800, Postal Station A,
5170 Yonge St., Willowdale, Ont. M2N 6J3

ROBERTA LEIGH

no time for marriage

Harlequin Books

TORONTO • NEW YORK • LONDON
AMSTERDAM • PARIS • SYDNEY • HAMBURG
STOCKHOLM • ATHENS • TOKYO • MILAN

I dedicate this book to Dora,
whose loyalty and loving care
of me has given me the peace of mind
to write.

Harlequin Presents first edition September 1985
ISBN 0-373-10819-2

Original hardcover edition published in 1985
by Mills & Boon Limited

CHAPTER ONE

SHARON KINGSTON looked across the desk at her employer and wondered if she had heard him correctly.

'You want me to go to *Thailand*?'

'Yes,' Mr Palmer replied. 'For six months. You'd be dividing your time between our hotels in Bangkok and Pattaya, which is a beachside resort. Providing you agree,' he added. 'I'll be sorry to lose you, but when Head Office asked me if I could recommend anyone to be our Liaison Officer there, I thought immediately of you.'

'Do you really think I can cope with the job?'

'Without question. You're the most able assistant I've had in years!'

Sharon smiled her pleasure at the compliment, but was still doubtful. 'My work there would be quite different from what I do here.'

'Easier, I should think. It's simply a matter of dealing with the various tour groups and handling their complaints and problems.'

'That should keep me busy night and day! It's tricky enough to do in England, but in the Far East . . .'

'Which is why we want someone like you to see the wheels turn smoothly. A high proportion of our tours come from America and their time schedules are tight. All you need is one aircraft arriving late, and you've a hundred guests on your hands for another night. Or else they don't arrive at all and a special dinner has to be written off! And that's apart from the routine problems.'

7

Sharon ran her fingers through her thick, corn-gold hair. 'I think you'd do better with a diplomat!'

'Hence my suggesting *you*,' Mr Palmer reiterated. 'You're our most promising management trainee, and if you do well out there, you'll be given charge of one of our smaller hotels on your return.'

A juicy carrot was being dangled before her, and Sharon's eyes—blue as summer skies—sparkled. Even in this so-called liberated era, women hotel managers were few and far between, and to be given charge of a hotel, no matter how small, would be a major step forward in her career.

'I know it's a serious decision for you,' the manager went on, 'but it's an important step in the right direction.'

'Putting it the way you have,' she murmured, 'I can hardly refuse.'

Mr Palmer came round the side of his desk to stand beside her. An ex-Naval officer, he had taken a paternal interest in her since reading in her Curriculum Vitae that her father had held the same rank as himself in the Second World War.

'You needn't give me your answer today,' he said benignly. 'Talk it over with someone first. Your boyfriend perhaps?'

'I don't have one,' Sharon said, and tried not to think of her last evening with Pete Wilburg nine months ago, when he had made it clear he was not yet ready to settle down, and that when he was, it wouldn't be with a career girl.

'When would I have to leave?' she asked.

'At the end of the month. You'll need a visa and innoculations, and a fair number of clothes. Thailand's hot and humid and you'll require several changes each day. We'll foot the bill, so don't penny pinch! You'll be mixing with the guests much more than you do here—making sure the special luncheons and dinners go off without a hitch, as well as occasionally joining them on our own Avonmore tours.'

'What about my accommodation?'

'You'll stay at the hotel.' Mr Palmer walked with her to the door. 'You've made a wise decision, Sharon. You won't regret going.'

Hoping he was right, Sharon spent the next ten days getting her visa, having her 'shots', and buying a summer wardrobe—no easy task early in January. But with a generous cheque in her purse she could afford to shop at the more expensive boutiques, whose customers, perennial sun worshippers with no money problems, expected and got high summer cottons in mid winter.

'What a lucky devil you are,' said an envious colleague. 'Thailand's fabulous this time of year. But make sure they send you home before the monsoon season.'

'It can't be worse than this,' Sharon commented, watching the rain streaming down the window.

'You obviously don't know Thailand. This is a drizzle compared with what you'll get there!'

'But at least it'll be warm! Just think. A week from now I'll be in a sleeveless dress dabbing away the perspiration!'

'As well as mosquitoes. It's not all roses, my lovely!'

'So it seems,' Sharon said dryly, and decided it would be as well to learn something of the country that was going to be her home for the next half year.

The Thai Information Office supplied her with pamphlets, maps, and a phrase book which she spent every available moment studying. She also read various tavel books which whetted her appetite about a land that, the more she learned of it, the more intriguing it seemed.

Her parents, who farmed in Scotland, were delighted when she telephoned them with news of her impending trip.

'It's time you saw more of the world,' her mother said. 'And this job's tailor made for you. You're a born smoother down of ruffled feathers!'

'Thai feathers may be rather more prickly! And American tourists definitely are!'

'You'll still manage it,' Mrs Kingston reiterated. 'But what are you doing with your apartment?'

Sharon looked around her small, Hampstead mews home. 'Sub-letting it to one of the girls in the office. Unless you and Dad would like it as a *pied-à-terre*?'

'Very funny,' her mother replied. 'I'm lucky if I can persuade your father to take me to Edinburgh once a year!'

'Any chance of *you* coming out to Bangkok?'

'I don't see why not. I'll see if I can work something out.'

'Marvellous,' Sharon enthused, knowing her mother would do no such thing. Her parents had an ideal marriage and loathed being apart from one another, even for a few days. Would she herself ever have such a relationship? At this stage in her life it seemed improbable. So far, the only men she had met who wanted marriage, were looking for full-time house-wives, and those who preferred career women, wanted them as live-in lovers.

Sighing, she went into the little kitchenette to make herself an omelette, then took it into the sitting room and switched on the television.

It was a year since she and Pete had met on a skiing holiday in Austria. Tall and slim, with a mop of unruly fair hair, he had looked devastating on the slopes, and swooningly handsome in the evening, when they had danced away the après ski hours.

He was a consultant engineer for an international construction company, and had spent most of his working life travelling, before being sent to London. His father was an American diplomat and his mother a Danish countess, and though he wasn't rich, he clearly came from a moneyed background.

Back in England, their friendship had flourished, and he had occasionally hinted he would like to settle down. But Sharon had always doubted his sincerity. She knew he was fond of her, loved her in his own way, but it was a fickle, here-today-gone-tomorrow love. Often he would not call her for weeks, claiming to be busy at work. Then there would be a spate of invitations, after which he'd drift away again.

Fortunately he had no idea how she felt about him, and she had even managed to hide it when he had told her his company were sending him to Japan for two years.

'I've had a fabulous time in England, thanks to you,' he said, looking down at her as they danced together at Annabel's, in Mayfair. 'I'll be in touch as soon as I'm settled, and we can meet up for another skiing holiday.'

She had known they wouldn't, though it had not lessened her hurt when he had not even sent her a postcard. For Pete, it was out of sight, out of mind, and though she had tried to do the same, it was proving a slow and painful process.

Three weeks after her interview with Mr Palmer, Sharon boarded a 747 for Bangkok. She was going via Abu Dhabi on the Arabian Gulf, flying time over fourteen hours. Until now, she had only gone on cheap package tours, but Avonmore had booked her first-class and she was thrilled by the unaccustomed luxury.

With suppressed excitement she watched as they

climbed through the clouds to reach the sky above, where a few stars had already begun twinkling on this late February afternoon. Shortly after take-off, a smiling Thai stewardess came round with free drinks and canapés of caviare and smoked salmon. She was tiny and slender, and emanated a gentle charm as she made her way gracefully through the cabin. 'I'd feel like an ox beside her,' Sharon thought wryly, momentarily regretting her five foot six inches and Raquel Welch proportions.

Opening her *Teach Yourself Thai*, she settled back to study it, nibbling on smoked salmon and sipping champagne. What a sybaritic way to acquire knowledge! She had found the language extremely difficult to learn, but was bravely battling on. Trouble was, one didn't only have to acquire a new vocabulary and lettering, but also different tones of voice, for the meaning of a word frequently depended on intonation. *Kao*, when spoken in varying ways, could be rice, old, they, or badly!

Fortifying herself with another glass of champagne, she continued with her studies for a further half hour before turning to a guide book and a potted résumé of the country's history. It had gained independence in 1939, and she was intrigued to find it had then changed its name from Siam—shades of Anna and the King—to 'Thai' land, which meant 'free'.

'More champagne?' the stewardess asked.

'Not unless you want me rolling in the aisle!'

Sharon set her glass on the table in front of her, feeling somewhat euphoric. It was a good thing the seat next to her was empty, for she was in no mood for small talk, or being chatted up by some business executive on an expense account trip. She'd had her fill of that in London! That had been one of the nice things about Pete. He had never come on strong nor tried to rush her into bed, and had laconically accepted her refusal to have an affair. Perhaps if she had given in to him ... But no. Sex would never have held him. He loved his freedom too much. And *she* loved her career, she reminded herself. It was far more important to her than marriage.

It was noon, local time next day, when they touched down at Don Muang Airport. The immigration building was like immigration buildings anywhere: large, modern and air-conditioned, its coolness welcome after the walk across the boiling tarmac. A polite official quickly checked her passport and visa, and minutes later she emerged into the Customs Hall.

As if on cue, a young boy in the dark-brown trousers and beige shirt of the Avonmore Group, rushed forward to take charge of her cases. The smile he gave the official was frankly conspiratorial, and Sharon guessed it was not luck alone that speeded her luggage through unopened. She had already learned from Head Office that the system of 'favours' was widespread throughout Asia.

'A case of "You scratch my back and I'll scratch yours",' one of her colleagues had said. 'It's marvellous as long as you have a back to scratch, but heaven help you if you don't!'

The boy piled her things into the back of a large shooting brake, and Sharon climbed in beside him as he took the wheel.

The road from the airport was wide and straight, like any British motorway, but there the resemblance ended, and she stared in fascination at the wooden houses perched on stilts and surrounded by palm trees. There was mile after mile of rice fields, with water buffalo wading through the mud and dragging ploughs behind them. It was the National Geographic come to life.

'My father is rice farmer,' the boy informed her. 'But I not like work on land.'

'My father's a farmer too,' Sharon smiled, 'but I never wanted to follow in his footsteps.'

'We not chip off old block!'

'We're certainly not,' she chuckled. 'Tell me, what's your name?'

'Is very long in Thai, so I shorten it to Ian.'

He swung the shooting brake off the main highway, and they bounced down a rutted road that ran beside a canal lined with shabby houses.

Sharon had read about these canals, or 'khlongs' as they were called here, which formed a network of waterways lacing the city, and was the reason Bangkok was called the 'Venice of the East'. But it had considerably less glamour, for the khlongs were not only the city's thoroughfares and water source, but drainage system too. No wonder Head Office had warned her to stick to mineral water!

They emerged from the side street into a bustling main road. Concrete and glass buildings contrasted with the timeless beauty of Buddhist temples; saffron-robed monks brushed against jean-clad youngsters; and American cars sped past 'samlors'—three-wheeled taxis with motor scooter engines. Despite the heavy flow of vehicles there were few traffic lights, and listening to the screech of brakes, Sharon decided that crossing the road meant taking your life in your hands!

'That's Jim Thompson's house.' Ian pointed left as they turned into Rama Road. 'He American architect and secret agent in Second World War. He settled here and made Thai silk famous. Then he go to Malaysia on vacation and not return. Murdered maybe.'

They had now reached the Chao Phraya River, a broad expanse of dull green water abounding with craft of every kind. People were milling along its banks, and though most of the men were in European suits, many women wore tight-fitting blouses with the traditional 'panung', a long, tightly wrapped skirt.

'My brother is monk,' Ian said, seeing her stare at an orange-robed young man, his head closely shaven. 'Every morning he walks through city with bowl, begging for food. He only allowed eat what he given.'

'Sounds a tough life,' she commented.

'He say he have better life next time.'

'Next time?' Sharon was puzzled.

Ian grinned. 'Buddhists believe in reincarnation!'

I wish I did, Sharon thought as the young man overtook a bus with reckless disregard for safety, and breathed a sigh of relief when he suddenly said:

'We nearly at Avonmore.'

Ian pointed ahead, but all she saw was a high white wall running parallel with the pavement for several hundred yards. A minute or two later they turned through an open pair of gilded wooden gates and bowled down a narrow tarmac road, with green lawns stretching either side of it. At the end of the drive rose a circular building some twenty storeys high, with a conical-shaped roof covered with slivers of glass which caught and reflected the light. The sparkling white building reminded her of a giant ice-cream; a welcome mirage, she thought, for many a hot and weary traveller!

'This most famous hotel in Bangkok.' Ian spoke as proudly as if he owned it. 'We have a little zoo, a ferry landing where you hire boat to go on river, and two roof restaurants. In big one you can order breakfast, lunch or dinner any time of day, so you can suit your "stomach clock"! Is good idea, eh?'

'Very,' she said, though privately thought it better to adapt one's body as quickly as possible. Yet come to think of it, it was seven a.m. in England now, and she would far rather have orange juice and coffee than steak and chips!

'Even animals not take notice of time difference,' Ian went on. 'Scientists take shellfish from East Coast America to California, but they still open and close shells like in eastern time zone.'

'Really?' She was intrigued. 'You're extremely knowledgeable, Ian.'

'I read much,' he said solemnly. 'All information useful. One day I manage big hotel too.'

Sharon could well believe it. He was a bright boy, with determination; the kind the Avonmore Group liked.

The shooting brake stopped outside the hotel entrance, and leaving Ian to see to her luggage, she went inside.

It was a relief to escape the oppressive heat, though the air-conditioned foyer struck her as being almost too cool. Marble floors stretched endlessly ahead, dotted with colourfully cushioned bamboo settees and armchairs. In the centre, a fountain cascaded into banks of tropical plants and flowers, the same blooms appearing in shiny golden bowls on the low, red-and-gold lacquered tables.

It was easy to spot the staff among the guests, for the women wore long, slim skirts and collarless jackets in brown and lemon, and the men light-weight brown suits. Within a moment of giving her name to one of them, she was shown to the office of Mr Bim, the Chinese manager.

Dapper and punctilious, he was the exact antithesis of Mr Palmer, but his smile was warm and he offered to take her on a quick tour of the hotel before showing her to her suite.

Although she would have preferred to shower and

change first, she tried to look enthusiastic as she followed him from one lavish reception room to another, all skilfully decorated in a subtle blend of East and West.

At the head of each staircase stood tubs of tropical flowers, and statues of Oriental deities glowed in the lamplit niches along the corridors. Despite the tropical clime, the upstairs floors were close-carpeted, and the bedroom windows draped with heavy Thai silk that matched the counterpanes on the modern divans. The bathrooms were ultra-modern, as was the beautifully made furniture in the more expensive suites.

Her own, on the tenth floor, was delightful, with a small balcony overlooking the river. Never had she seen such a wondrous sight. A panorama of golden temple spires stretched before her, their undulating roofs glittering with colourful mosaic tiles, while below lay the broad green ribbon of water, crowded with barges, motor boats and water-buses.

'It's beautiful,' she murmured. 'And so is the hotel.'

'We like to think so,' Mr Bim said, 'though some guests are never satisfied. They blame us for the noise on the river, as well as the mosquitoes!'

Sharon laughed. 'What shall I say to them when they do?'

'I'll leave *you* to think up the answer!' came the smiling reply. 'I've been told by Head Office that you're a born diplomat, so I'm sure you'll handle all contingencies admirably, Miss Kingston.'

It was on the tip of her tongue to ask him to call her Sharon, when she remembered Eastern protocol, and that he should be allowed to unbend in his own time. But his friendliness warmed her, and she was sure they would work well together, once she had grown used to all the different customs.

'Take it easy for the rest of the day,' Mr Bim

ordered as he went to the door. 'Catch up on your sleep and start work tomorrow.'

Left alone, Sharon unpacked, then poured herself a glass of pineapple juice kept in the small refrigerator that stood in one corner, before stepping on to the balcony. What a romantic place this was. It would have been wonderful to spend a holiday here with Pete. Damn! She had promised herself not to think of him, yet here she was doing exactly that. It was about time she consigned him to limbo land and concentrated on her career.

It might not be as emotionally satisfying, but it would not let you down and it didn't have a roving eye!

CHAPTER TWO

SHARON found no difficulty in settling down. The staff were polite and friendly, and though they might have disagreements among themselves, did not show it in her presence.

Her first few days were spent learning the running of the hotel. In many respects it was similar to the London Avonmore, the main difference being that the guests here were tourists rather than business executives, and consequently more demanding about their comforts.

'It's often the little things that cause the most friction,' Mr Bim told her one morning as she sipped iced coffee in his office.

'What are the main complaints?' she asked.

'It differs with the nationalities. Americans want iced water with everything, Germans like large pillows, and Italians expect rice or pasta with every meal.'

'Well at least rice shouldn't be a problem!' she grinned. 'Which reminds me, I promised to let the chef give me a tour of the kitchens this morning.'

'Then don't keep him waiting. You know how temperamental chefs can be!'

Heeding the advice, Sharon went off to see him. Crossing the foyer, eye-catching in a cinnamon brown cotton skirt and crisp lemon blouse with frilled neckline, she came in for many admiring glances. No shortage here of dates, should she want them, for a large contingent of engineering executives—all competing for a highly lucrative highway building contract—had been semi-permanent residents for months. Pausing briefly to chat to one or two of them, she was only a few minutes late for her meeting with Mr Kei, the tubby, ebullient Chinese who ruled over the four cavern-like rooms which made up the kitchen. He had learned his English in Hong Kong and was plainly happy to show it off, for he talked non-stop on his 'Cook's Tour'!

'We do many cuisines here,' he informed her proudly, 'but Thai food is our speciality.'

A delicious smell of garlic, chillies and dried shrimps came from the simmering sauces, while huge cauldrons of rice and noodles stood alongside copper pans filled with finger-sized corn cobs, courgettes no longer than one's little finger, and lobsters from the Indian ocean.

'Twice a week we have buffet luncheons on the terrace,' he went on. 'And chefs from other hotels come to see what we're serving!'

Sharon could well believe it, and on her way back to Reception made a note to sample a buffet lunch herself. For the rest of the day she intended dealing with the guests, and what better place to start than where they checked in?

Her initiation began at once, with a Mr and Mrs Vandencart, an American couple who were displeased with their room.

'We can let you have a larger one,' Sharon placated them, 'but it will cost you more. At the moment you have the best one within your price range.'

'Well, I don't intend paying a cent extra,' Mr Vandencart, a tall, spare man in a seersucker suit, stated flatly. 'My travel agent assured me I'd be getting a suite—not an ordinary room.'

'Then your agent was lying.' Sharon tempered her

bluntness with a smile. 'He knew precisely what your accommodation was, and agreed it. I'm afraid we can't be held responsible for him. As a successful business man, I'm sure you appreciate our position.'

She had no idea how successful Mr Vandencart was, but believed firmly in the power of flattery, and was delighted to see it working yet again, for the man swelled with self-importance.

'If I ran my business the way Pixley Tours do theirs, I'd lose every one of my customers!'

'Perhaps if you told Mr Pixley he'd take the hint!'

'That's precisely what I'll do.' Gripping his wife's arm he was about to move off when Sharon heard him give an exclamation.

'Well I'll be danged! Look, Betsy! There's Kane Morgan. I'd no idea he was in Bangkok.'

They hurried over to a tall, dark-haired man in his mid thirties, who had emerged from one of the elevators. His formal grey suit told Sharon he was no holidaymaker, but her speculation was cut short by an irate German complaining his hired driver was demanding a large tip before taking him out for the day.

It took a while to arrange another car for him, but when he had departed and she again glanced over to the Vandencarts, they were still talking to Kane Morgan. Even from a distance she sensed that the smile on his face was forced, and from the way he jiggled the coins in his pocket she was positive he couldn't wait to escape. Idly she watched him. He was handsome in a hawkish way, with a thin, tanned face and aquiline nose. He was too far away for her to make out the colour of his eyes beneath the thick, expressive brows, but there was no ignoring the wide, firm mouth and aggressive jawline.

She was wondering if he was American, when she

heard him say goodbye, his accent clipped and decidedly British.

'I hope you're free to have a meal with us one evening?' Mrs Vandencart trilled.

'May I let you know? I'm here on business, and that gets priority I'm afraid.' With a smile he strode off, skirting the Reception Desk and giving Sharon a cursory glance.

For a split second she found herself looking into dark blue eyes of such steel-like intensity it took her breath away—though she was piqued he didn't appear to notice her at all, for there was no flicker in his face as he passed her. So what? she told herself, and from the corner of her eye watched him stop to speak to a porter, towering above him so that he had to bend his head to hear what the man said. His hair was as black as the Thai's, but more glossy, and as he lifted a hand to smooth it back, she glimpsed the flash of a narrow gold watch.

Another rush of guests brought her back to her duties, and it was nearly lunch time before she had a chance to talk to Mr Bim about the Vandencarts.

'If Pixley Tours won't help I'd still let them have another room,' he advised. 'Vandencart's a frequent visitor here on business, though this is the first time he's come on vacation. I suppose he took a package tour because he thought they'd arrange his itinerary better than he could himself.'

'There are quite a few businessmen here,' she commented. 'Who's Kane Morgan?'

'One of our best clients. Stays here at least three times a year.' Mr Bim half-turned in his chair, giving Sharon a view of the wide, continually watered lawns behind him. 'He's been here a month already, and always has one of the penthouse suites. He's head of Morgan Construction Company.'

It was a world-wide organisation and she was impressed. 'He's young for such a position.'

Mr Bim nodded. 'He's competing for the highway project, as a matter of fact, so he'll be here another month at least. Probably two. Some of the biggest firms are tendering for it, and Mr Bonlam—the Minister—is delaying his decision in the hope of forcing them to lower their prices.'

'I'd hate having to compete that way,' Sharon commented.

'So would I. But when millions of dollars are involved, a saving of even half a per cent amounts to a fortune.'

'Can Thailand afford such an ambitious building programme?'

'It cannot afford not to. Highways are essential for progress, and progress raises living standards and puts money in people's pockets. A contented country is less likely to go Communist, you know, and with the kind of neighbours we have—who are always looking for a chance to create dissension here—we have to be watchful.'

Reluctant to enter into a political discussion, Sharon politely excused herself. She had the afternoon free and wanted to explore the city.

She had not left the hotel since her arrival, and after a light lunch of salad and fruit, she climbed into a taxi, all set to enjoy herself. Slowly it moved alongside the Chao Phraya River, which as usual was bustling with a vast armada of working craft. She was intrigued by the women, in their conical straw hats, who were unloading fruit and vegetables from long, shallow boats. And what an enormous variety there was: pineapples, oranges, melons, bananas no bigger than one's thumb, mangoes, reddish-purple mangosteens, prickly durians and large green and orange pawpaws.

In the side-streets dozens of outdoor stalls were selling food, though equally as much produce was set out on the ground, under large parasols. The heat was overwhelming and there were mosquitoes everywhere. No wonder the market women carried fly-whisks!

A party of Italian tourists—expensive cameras slung from their necks—caught her eye as they haggled over prices. The contrast between them and the gentle-spoken Thais was striking. How easy it was for the affluent to forget the poverty around them when they returned to the luxury of their air-conditioned hotels. Did Kane Morgan ever think of this? she wondered, and couldn't imagine him giving thought to anything except business. He probably believed that by providing modern highways he was helping the Thais on their way to prosperity. But why pick on poor Mr Morgan? Was she still piqued because he had not noticed her this morning?

Surprisingly, he was almost the first person she saw later that evening as she took her place at a side table on the terrace, for dinner. He was already there, accompanied by a middle-aged Thai man. A few minutes later they were joined by two women, one in her fifties and the other considerably younger and extremely beautiful. Slim as a wand, she was unusually tall for her race, with jet black hair looped into a coil on the nape of her neck. Her dark eyes were enormous beneath well-shaped brows, and her delicate nose flared slightly at the nostrils, giving her a disdainful look echoed by the pouting, sensuous mouth. Her traditional cheomsang drew attention to the subtle curves of her body, and the diamonds twinkling in her ears and around her narrow wrist, proclaimed both money and taste. Kane Morgan seemed to like her, and they sat close together as they studied the menu.

Afraid of being caught staring at them, Sharon concentrated on her own, choosing Tom Yam Gung— a popular Thai soup—to start with. It contained prawns and chicken, and was flavoured with soy sauce, tiny red peppers and lemon juice.

'Do you know the people dining with Mr Morgan?' she asked the waiter as he wrote down her order.

'Is Mr Bonlam and family,' he said, without glancing in their direction. 'We all hope Mr Morgan get contract. He excellent guest here and staff like him.'

So does Mr Bonlam's daughter, Sharon thought, watching the way the girl made up to him during the meal. Not that she received any discouragement from the Englishman, for he didn't seem able to take his eyes off her. Was it genuine attraction or expediency? she wondered. Men of his type were probably used to women throwing themselves at him, though not all had the advantage of a father who could hand out a billion-dollar contract!

They were still at table when Sharon left the terrace and went into the American bar for coffee. Everyone around here was with someone, and not unnaturally she felt dispirited at being alone. In England it had never bothered her, for she had returned to her own home each night. But living in this luxurious holiday atmosphere, her single state made her feel like a fish out of water. It was an emotion she had to overcome; if she didn't, her stay here would be an unhappy one.

Depressed, she returned to her room and settled herself on the balcony, switching off the lights so as not to attract insects. A full moon lit up the temple spires across the river, and briefly she wondered if Kane Morgan and the beautiful Miss Bonlam were out walking in the moonlight. What if they were? she chided herself. She should count herself lucky she was here at all, not waste time envying anyone else. A year from now she might be managing her own hotel, and that would be far more rewarding than being someone's temporary girlfriend.

On which determinedly optimistic thought she left the balcony and went to bed.

CHAPTER THREE

THE next few days found Sharon still vaguely depressed, the sight of so many happy holidaymakers doing nothing to elevate her mood. Husbands and wives contented in their togetherness; lovers luxuriating in their surroundings and in each other; carefree groups enjoying the camaraderie of shared pleasure, made her realise how alone she was, and what little recompense a career was for loneliness. Yet surely it was possible to combine marriage and a worthwhile job? To find a man who would be happy to have a wife with ambition for herself as well as *him*? It was foolish to think all men were like Pete.

Mulling over all he had said, she knew she had been naive to think love would change him. He had been so determined to stay free, he had not *allowed* himself to care for her. But it was pointless harking back to the past. They had broken up and she must concentrate on her future. If these six months were successful, she would be well on her way up the promotion ladder.

Despite long hours, her job was not arduous, though it was frequently trying. Experienced travellers felt their know-how gave them the right to demand the best—regardless of whether they had booked it—and inexperienced ones fell prey to crooked shopkeepers, cheating taxi drivers, and tummy bugs—and blamed the hotel for them all!

From time to time Sharon saw Kane Morgan striding through the lobby. He was always accompanied by men: solemn Thais, portly Europeans or lanky Americans. She never saw him smile and wondered how the negotiations were going. Mr Bonlam had still not made a decision, and she heard rumours that the contract wouldn't be finalised until more foreign aid was forthcoming.

Some two weeks after she had settled in, she decided to take an early morning dip in the pool. On the one occasion she had ventured in during the afternoon, so many guests had taken the opportunity to air their grievances to her, she had felt she was back at her desk in Reception! But at seven in the morning it was deserted, and she padded across the grass and dropped her wrap and towel on a white wood lounging chair.

It was only as she straightened that she heard splashing, and she moved quickly behind a cluster of spiky green bushes. From this vantage point all she could see was the deep end, but as she watched, a man swam into view and climbed out. Raking his hand through his wet hair, he stretched his frame upon the grass. He was a superb example of muscular strength and fitness: broad chest, slim hips and strong, sinewy arms and legs. There was something familiar about his movements, but it was only when he turned his head that she saw it was Kane Morgan.

Unaccountably embarrassed, she decided to give up her swim. He looked so relaxed he might regard her presence as an intrusion on his privacy—or else think she had come here deliberately to scrape acquaintance with him! Stealthily creeping out from behind the bushes, she tiptoed over to collect her wrap and towel.

'I hope I'm not frightening you away?'

A deep male voice made Sharon spin round, the towel dropping to the ground as she saw Kane Morgan, half-sitting-up watching her. The man must have eyes in the back of his head!

'No, you're not,' she lied. 'I—er—it's later than I thought.'

'It always is,' came the dry answer, and he sat up fully and surveyed her.

Instantly Sharon was aware of her scant attire, and felt the colour run up under her skin. It was one thing to wear a bikini on the beach, surrounded by others dressed in similar vein, but quite different to be the sole object of a pair of steel blue eyes. Yet she would not give him the satisfaction of knowing he had embarrassed her, and she slowly picked up her towel from the floor and held it in her hand.

'Are you holidaying here?' he asked unexpectedly.

Piqued that he did not recognise her—after all he had passed her several times when she had been serving at Reception, and she was also the only European there—an imp of mischief decided her to string him along.

'My whole life's a holiday,' she said lightly. 'What about you?'

'I'm one of the world's workers. But then I don't have your advantages.'

'Advantages?'

'Of being a stunning natural blonde.'

'Thanks for the compliment. But how do you know it isn't from a bottle?'

'Because your outfit doesn't leave much to the imagination!' His eyes dropped to her ringless hands. 'How long have you been here?'

'Ages,' she said with deliberate vagueness.

'With a boyfriend?'

What a nerve he had! Did he think good-looking women incapable of existing without a man?

'Certainly not,' she flashed. 'I'm here alone.'

'Indeed.'

There was a wealth of meaning in the word, as in the raising of one dark eyebrow, and Sharon longed to kick him where it would hurt most. Unaware of her thoughts, Kane Morgan rose to his feet in one lithe movement and came towards her.

'I'm alone too,' he smiled, 'so how about joining me for breakfast?'

'You don't let the grass grow under your feet, do you?'

'No. If I see something I want, I try to get it. You can't sit back and wait for something to happen.'

He was now so close to her she could smell the warmth of him; a musky, vibrant scent that made her startlingly aware of his masculinity. She stepped back from him, and though she was a tall girl, she had to tilt her head to look into his face. Close to, he was even better looking, his eyes sparkling with health and vigour, his hair shiny as satin. But it in no way lessened her dislike of his behaviour.

'I'm afraid I never eat breakfast,' she drawled. 'So I'll have to turn down your invitation.'

'Dinner then?'

Sharon hid her surprise. From what she had gleaned about him, she had expected him to spend all his free time with Tassy Bonlam. Which showed how naive she still was! After all, she had been in the hotel business long enough to know that Kane Morgan's behaviour was typical of so many jet-setting business men who lived for their work and regarded the female of the species as expendable sex objects to be picked up and discarded at will.

'I don't eat dinner either—with men I don't know,' she said.

'We can easily remedy that,' he replied. 'I'm Kane Morgan, and I'm well known to the management of this hotel, who can vouch for my integrity—I don't make a booking unless I intend to keep it; my honesty—I always pay my bar bills—and my single status.'

'You mean no woman has snapped you up?' Sharon questioned with simulated astonishment.

'Nor likely too,' he grinned. 'I like variety of choice!'

'Me too,' she replied. 'And you're not the variety *I* would choose.'

Before he could reply, she turned on her heel and walked away, chuckling inwardly at his look of astonishment.

Only when she was changing to go down to Reception, did Sharon's amusement turn to concern. Kane Morgan was a guest here, and if he wished he could make life difficult for her. Yet somehow she felt he was too sophisticated to do that. Besides, for every girl who turned him down, there were probably a hundred who wouldn't, and though her attitude might have surprised him, she was pretty sure he would have forgotten all about her before the day was through.

Later that morning, as she was sorting out the problem of a double booking for the penthouse suite in the west wing, she saw him again. Casual in slacks and T-shirt, he was showing a map to a tour guide, a middle-aged woman with whom he seemed to be having a serious conversation. The change in his demeanour was astonishing. Gone was the bantering sophisticate with the sardonic expression and 'come to bed' eyes, in its place an intelligent man with a warm, friendly expression. Yet the good looks and superb physique were the same, as was the energy and vitality he exuded; and it was this which set him apart from the rest of the men Sharon had met.

Although Kane Morgan's behaviour by the pool had irritated her, her curiosity to know more about him prompted her to quiz one of the clerks when she lunched with him in the staff canteen that day.

'Mr Morgan seems to be staying here a long time,' she murmured casually.

'I don't think he will leave until Mr Bonlam has made a decision about the contract,' Mr Chittiwera told her. 'But he often flies back to London. Last time the Minister's daughter went with him. They are—how you say?—good friends.'

Sharon was not surprised. 'She's very beautiful.'

'So are you,' the young clerk said shyly. 'Our sunshine agrees with you.'

Sharon accepted the compliment with a smile. Although she spent much of her time indoors, she had still managed to acquire a slight tan, and her corn-coloured hair glinted with sun-silvered lights. Today she had discarded her usual skirt and blouse for a cotton dress a shade deeper than her blue eyes, the manager having surprised her yesterday by saying she could wear her own clothes if she wished; an offer she had immediately taken up.

'Does Miss Bonlam work?' she asked.

'Not officially. She's a graduate of the Harvard Business School, and rumour says her father relies a great deal upon her advice.'

Could that be part of her attraction for Kane Morgan? Sharon wondered cynically. He looked the type to love judiciously.

'I'm surprised Mr Morgan finds time for a girlfriend,' she said aloud. 'He seems to work non-stop—except for his morning swim.'

'He hardly ever relaxes,' Mr Chittiwera agreed, piling his plate with fried noodles. 'He is a man who always likes to be in control of himself.'

'And everybody else, I should think,' Sharon quipped, recollecting the jutting jaw, and was inexplicably curious to know whether he was like that with Tassy, too. Hastily she pushed the thought aside, irritated to find it was leading to sensual ones that she wanted no part of.

Yet these same images returned later that afternoon when she went to the mezzanine floor to organise a cocktail party for fifty guests, and saw Tassy and her father going into one of the conference suites with several dark-suited men. They couldn't be meeting Kane Morgan, for the Englishman had left the hotel at midday, and she was curious to know if this meant he was no longer favourite for the contract? If so, would he and the Thai girl no longer be 'good friends', or was her attraction for him stronger than business ties?

She was still musing on this when she returned to the lobby, where she was immediately pounced upon by an agitated blonde woman in her middle thirties, who was holding on to a mischievous-looking boy of about eight.

'I wonder if you could look after Terry for me?' she pleaded. 'I'm due at the hairdresser's in five minutes and my husband promised to be back to look after him. But he hasn't arrived and Terry doesn't want to come with me.'

'How long will you be?' Sharon asked.

'About an hour. Then I'm meeting someone for tea at the Oriental Hotel. But my husband's bound to be back by then.'

And if he isn't, Sharon thought cynically, I'll be expected to babysit all afternoon.

'I'm afraid I can only keep an eye on him,' she explained. 'I have to take over at the Reception Desk now.'

'I'll be quick as I can,' the woman promised. 'You're an angel to help me. I'm Mrs Victorsen by the way, and my husband really *should* be back any moment. I'm not making it up.' She pulled her son forward. 'Now be a good boy, Terry, and don't give the young lady any trouble.'

For the first five minutes Terry obeyed his mother's command. Then boredom set in and he started racing around the foyer, sliding across the marble floor and jumping over the low-back chairs. Twice Sharon was forced to give him chase and order him back to his seat, but the third time it was Mr Bim—returning from an appointment—who caught hold of him and frog-marched him back to her.

'This young man tells me you're supposed to be playing with him,' he stated.

'Not until I'm free. He knows that.' In a low voice she explained what had happened, and the Manager, though mollified, was still annoyed.

'We can't have him rushing around upsetting the guests, Miss Kingston. Take him into the garden and I'll get someone to stand in for you here.'

Wishing it were the other way around, Sharon thanked him and led the boy out. Instantly they were enveloped by stifling heat, a shock after the air-conditioned lobby.

'I want an ice cream,' Terry stated, pulling off his cotton T-shirt.

Sharon shook her head, not relishing the idea of having him run riot in the American ice-cream bar.

'Then I want to go and swim,' he said.

'You'll have to wait for your father. I have to go back on duty as soon as he comes for you, and there isn't time for me to fetch my swim suit.'

'You can sit on the side and watch me.'

'And what happens if I have to dive in and rescue you?'

Terry giggled at the idea, and taking advantage of his good humour, Sharon suggested they had a quick peep at the animals in the little zoo at the far end of the garden.

The boy agreed, and chatted away cheerily as they

walked over the thick, springy grass, past clumps of colourful tropical vines, pink hibiscus bushes, and beds filled with roses. On the west side of the gardens, away from the river, they came to a fenced-in enclosure which held parakeets, monkeys and a baby elephant.

Terry watched intrigued as the monkeys scrambled up and down their cages, or sat on wooden ledges and busily ate nuts, ignoring the brightly coloured birds that flew around them, their noisy cries disturbing the languid peace of the sultry afternoon.

'My Daddy says you can see elephants pulling logs and bathing in the river near Chiang Mei,' he announced. 'He's going to take me there soon.'

'I'm sure you'll have a wonderful time,' Sharon smiled. 'You're from England, aren't you?' she went on, to keep the conversation going.

'Yes. I live in Bromley. Daddy's a very important businessman, and travels round the world. But Mummy doesn't like it 'cos she gets lonely at home.'

'But you've both come with him on this trip,' Sharon said diplomatically, 'so she isn't lonely any longer.'

'We only came 'cos I was ill and the doctor said I needed a holiday,' Terry informed her, then ran his fingers along the bars of one of the cages, startling a parakeet into screeching anger.

Deciding a change of venue was called for, Sharon led the boy to a wooden seat in the shade of a coconut palm.

'Let's play "I Spy",' she suggested. 'You go first.'

Terry dangled sun-burnt legs over the edge of the bench, and thought deeply. 'You won't guess this one,' he said confidently. 'I spy with my little eye something beginning with "S".'

'Sun.'

'No.'

'Sandal.'

'No.'

'Shrub.'

'No, no!' he squealed in delight.

'Oh dear, you've got me stumped.'

'It's sup-pa-rod.'

'What's that?'

'Thai for pineapple. Look, they're groeing over there.'

'That wasn't very fair,' Sharon demurred. 'We should stick to English words. I hardly know any Thai.'

'I won't play then.' Jumping down from the bench, he disappeared into the shrubbery.

Sharon followed hard on his heels but couldn't see him anywhere.

'Terry!' she called. 'Come on out and we'll play a different game.' There was no answer and she delved deeper into the undergrowth.

'Boo!'

She almost jumped out of her skin as he appeared from behind a bush, then raced off again, weaving between the shrubs and imitating a racing car.

'Terry, come back!' she called. 'Let's go inside and I'll buy you an ice-cream.'

'Don't want one.'

He disappeared once more, and the next thing she heard was a loud crash and an angry male voice exploding with a word that brought colour to her cheeks.

Fearing heaven knew what, she pushed her way through the bushes, stopping aghast as, ahead of her, in a clearing, she saw Terry face down on the grass. A small table was overturned beside him, documents were strewn everywhere, and a dark-haired man was crawling about on the ground retrieving them.

Kane Morgan!

'Terry!' Sharon rushed towards the child, who was now on his knees. 'Are you hurt?'

'He's fine,' the man snapped. 'Though I'm not sure *I* am.' He stood up on the last word and suddenly saw her face to face. 'Well, well, so we meet again.' His smile was anything but pleasant and she returned it nervously.

'I'm terribly sorry for what's happened. Terry's a bit high-spirited and——'

'A bit?' came the furious exclamation. 'In my opinion you should keep him on a lead!'

'He didn't knock into you on purpose,' she protested, and bent to pick up some of the papers.

'Leave them,' Kane Morgan snapped. 'They're private.'

'I wasn't going to read them,' she replied coldly. 'I was merely trying to help.'

'You'd do better helping your charge learn his manners. As a Nanny, you'd make a first-class vet!'

'And as a gentleman you'd make a first-class boar!'

'Except that *I* wasn't the one charging around.'

'You can't expect an eight-year-old to behave like a middle-aged man!' she said sweetly, hiding her amusement that he should think her a children's nanny. She saw Kane Morgan's eyes glint with anger. Being somewhere in his middle thirties, he probably took her remark personally. Well, serve him right! His anger was totally out of proportion to the inconvenience he had suffered.

'Children should be taught that a hotel isn't their own home,' he went on remorselessly.

'Nor is it a prison.' She stepped back from him. He was casually clad in slacks and open-neck shirt, and she was aware of his bronzed skin and the warmth that emanated from it. He was like a beautifully coordinated panther, perfectly controlled but ready to spring.

'If you were a father, you'd be more understanding,' she went on. 'Children need freedom, not to be hedged in by unnecessary rules.'

'You consider good manners unnecessary? Your charge was crashing around like a young bull!'

'He's in a garden for heaven's sake! You can't expect him to sit and twiddle his thumbs.'

'If he were in *my* charge,' came the icy rejoinder, 'he'd have trouble sitting down at all!'

'Physical violence resolves nothing,' she said derisively. 'But you obviously see *everything* in terms of the physical!'

Grasping Terry's hand, she quickly pulled him out of Kane Morgan's sight. It was only as she did, that the full impact of her behaviour hit her. Their meeting at the poolside had been a purely personal encounter, and he could not complain to anyone about it. But this one was different, and if he told Mr Bim about Terry, she could well find herself in for a reprimand. Like it or not, she would have to seek Mr Morgan out later in the day, and eat humble pie—two portions probably— but for the moment it would do him good to brood on what she had said.

Terry was still quiet from his fall and kept stopping to touch his knees.

'They're only scratches,' she consoled, 'I'll sponge off the dirt, and you'll be right as rain.'

'I'd like to go back and knock down his silly old chair again,' he said defiantly.

'He might knock *you* down in return,' she scolded. 'You've done enough damage for one day, my lad. We'd better go and see if your mother's finished with the hairdresser.'

Mrs Victorsen was emerging from the salon as they

returned to the lobby, looking prettier and more relaxed after an hour free of her son, though her face fell as she saw Sharon's expression.

'What's Terry been up to now?'

'He was running and he fell over and scratched his legs.'

'Oh dear.' Mrs Victorsen put her arm round her son's shoulder. 'Did you hurt yourself, darling?'

'I'm fine,' he said, pushing her away. 'I ran into a table and knocked over a man sitting there.'

'Oh, Terry, I hope you didn't hurt him?' Mrs Victorsen looked so worried, Sharon took pity on her.

'Nothing terrible happened. The table will recover, and so will Mr Morgan.'

'Mr Morgan! Don't tell me it was *his* table.' The woman paled significantly. 'That's dreadful. My husband works for him. I hope you said you were sorry, Terry?'

The little boy shook his head. 'I didn't know who he was.'

'Mr Morgan didn't know Terry either,' Sharon added quickly.

'Oh.' There was a pause then, and a faint smile warmed the harassed features. 'Well, let's hope he doesn't find out the truth! I'd better keep this little monster out of his sight.'

Out of mine too, Sharon thought, and thankfully returned to the comparative quiet of the Reception Desk.

'You look as if you've had a hard time!' Mr Chittiwera commented, grinning.

'Just a drama with our most important guest! Anything exciting happen here?'

'It's about to. Fifty Swedes are arriving in half an hour and none of their rooms are ready.'

Sharon stared into his face. 'You serious?'

'Regrettably, yes. Mathewson Tours checked out two hours late—their flight was delayed and they didn't vacate their rooms until noon—by which time the chambermaids had gone to lunch.'

Furious no one had told her of this before, Sharon dashed for the elevator, narrowly missing Kane Morgan, who was emerging.

'I can see where your charge gets his behaviour from,' he murmured, and strode on towards the coffee shop.

Cheeks burning, Sharon went into the elevator and pressed the button with a shaky hand. What a hateful man he was!

But all thoughts of him vanished when she stepped out at the tenth floor and saw the choas of the bedrooms.

'Everything that can go wrong, *has* gone wrong,' Mrs Kung, the housekeeper cried, in a state of near-panic. 'Three of the washing machines aren't working and clean sheets won't be available until later this afternoon.'

'Don't we have any extra stock?'

'A room full. But Mr Bim has the keys, and he's gone to Pattaya and won't be back till tomorrow morning.'

'Isn't there another key?'

'No. Mr Bim likes to control all the stock himself.'

Silently vowing this was one duty he would have to abandon, Sharon asked the woman to take her to the stock room.

'And tell one of the maids to get a maintenance man to meet me there. We'll have to break the lock.'

'I daren't do that!' Mrs Kung was horrified.

'I'm not asking you to,' Sharon placated. 'I'll take full responsibility myself. But we can't have fifty guests waiting in the lobby all afternoon.'

Within a quarter of an hour the store room lock was forced open, sufficient linen removed, and the door sealed again, with the man instructed to put on a new lock and provide two new keys.

'I'll lay on a special tea for the Swedes,' she told Mrs Kung as they returned to the elevator. 'That should keep them downstairs an extra hour, which will give you time to finish preparing the rooms.'

Tearfully thanking her, the housekeeper hurried away, then suddenly and rushed back.

'Some Americans have checked into the East penthouse, and I have to see they have everything they require. That's one rule I daren't break.'

'I'll do it,' Sharon promised. 'You stay on this floor and get things organised.'

It was the first time since her tour of the hotel, that Sharon had been to the penthouse floor. The decor was far more sumptuous than the lower floors, with crimson carpeting in the corridors and Oriental rugs in the suites. The Dixons, who had just arrived in the East penthouse, were in the middle of unpacking, and assured her they were delighted with everything so far.

'If you've any particular requests, please let us know,' Sharon said, relieved *something* was going well for her today. 'Then next time you stay with us, they'll have been noted in our "specials" book.'

'A specials book? What a marvellous idea.' Mrs Dixon's chuckle was as warm and friendly as her appearance. 'I bet it's pages thick!'

'It is,' Sharon agreed. 'But our guests appreciate it.' She looked at Mr Dixon—as thin as his wife was plump—who was on the phone ordering his particular brand of bourbon.

'You won't have to do that on your next visit,' she added. 'Your favourite brand will be ready in the fridge for you!'

'Alongside with Thai dancing girls?'

'I'll check with your wife first!'

Smiling, she left them, and was stepping into the elevator when a man's voice called out for her to hold it for him.

The hair on the nape of her neck prickled as she recognised Kane Morgan's voice, and her heart thumped erratically as she kept her finger on the 'hold' button until he joined her. Carefully she avoided his eyes as he entered. She knew she owed him an apology but the words stuck in her throat. He had been so rude, he didn't deserve one. Yet he was a guest and she an employee, as he was bound to find out, and it was her duty—as she had already told herself—to eat humble pie.

Cautiously she shifted her position so she could see him out of the corner of her eyes. He was formally dressed now, in a light grey suit with a white silk shirt and club tie. His expression was formal too; wide, well-shaped mouth firmly closed, eyes hooded by half-lowered lids, giving the impression he was totally unaware of her presence.

'I'm s-sorry about this afternoon,' she stammered, hoping he would not snap her head off. 'Children can b-be a nuisance, I know. I hope you managed to sort out your papers?'

'Yes,' he said brusquely. 'But in future, take better care of your charge.'

'He isn't. My charge, I mean. I was only looking after him for the afternoon.' She took a deep breath. 'Actually I—er—I work here.'

'Really? Not in public relations I hope?'

Sharon went scarlet. 'Not quite. Though part of my job is to make sure all our guests are happy here.'

'I hope you succeed better with the other guests than you've done with me.'

It was an ungracious reply and she swallowed her anger. 'What happened with Terry was wrong. That's why I'm offering you an apology, Mr Morgan. But as to our own conversation by the pool ... well, I'm certainly not apologising for *that*.'

'Was it insulting to invite you to have breakfast or dinner with me?'

'Not if that was all you had meant,' she said bluntly. 'But it was quite clear you considered me easy game.'

'Oh come now,' he expostulated. 'You're a beautiful young woman and I thought you were staying here alone. So what nicer than to ask you out?'

'It was the way you did it. I don't blame you, Mr Morgan. I blame all the girls who've obviously said "yes" to you!'

'I've never needed to put a gun to their heads,' he replied silkily.

'I'm sure not.' She made herself look him up and down in the time-honoured way that men did women, and saw from the gleam in his eye that he was aware of what she was doing. 'You're a handsome hunk of man, Mr Morgan, and a woman who didn't want more than that, might find you very satisfying. But I am not one of them.'

'As you've already said. But you can't condemn me for trying. If one succeeds with a hundred, one cannot be blamed for believing one will succeed with a hundred and one.'

Her eyes flashed fury. 'You're insufferable!'

'It isn't *my* behaviour that's at fault—it's today's woman. She wants to be treated as an equal, and when she is, she objects.'

'Regarding someone as a sex object isn't treating them as an equal.'

'You misunderstand me. The liberated female wants total honesty about sexual relationships—and that's what I believe in too. You are exceptionally fanciable, and I made no pretence about it. However, you are clearly not liberated, and I apologise.'

'I'm a darn sight more liberated than you,' Sharon stormed. 'I don't look at a man and think only in terms of bed!'

'Nor do I,' he said. 'But I can't help thinking it when I see a beautiful woman!'

Her reply was cut short by the elevator stopping to let in another couple, and Sharon moved back into the corner, glad she had been prevented from saying any more. From now on she would avoid Kane Morgan like the plague. If she didn't, he could well cause the death of her job with the Avonmore Group.

CHAPTER FOUR

KANE MORGAN stifled a yawn and looked at his watch. The meeting at the Ministry had dragged on for three hours, and looked like continuing for three more if he didn't call a halt. Bonlam had been called away to see the Prime Minister and had assigned his deputy to take over—an earnest young man determined to prove to his superiors how thorough he was, which was resulting in every specification being meticulously re-analysed.

Kane's quick mind had soon found this unutterably boring. His attention began to wander and his temper—quick at the best of times—was becoming difficult to control. But he had trained himself to keep it in check—in a work situation that is—he thought wryly, remembering yesterday afternoon's debacle in the garden. This self-discipline had made him—in the short space of ten years—head of one of the largest construction companies in the world, the bulk of his business being with governments, and Lord knew what self-control *that* required!

But this deal looked like needing the most. No sooner was one tricky problem behind him, than another reared its head. And now, to cap it all, he had heard rumours that Bonlam was out of favour with the Prime Minister, and his deputy might be given his job.

Kane inched his wrist forward and saw it was five forty-five. Unless he called a halt, this man would drone on interminably. Rustling his papers together, he said coolly: 'Mr Bonlam's been in possession of all the extra costings for more than a month. I've discussed them with him at length and see no purpose in going over them again.'

From the corner of his eye he saw Mark Victorsen smother a smile, and gave him a warning stare. Instantly Victorsen became poker-faced, and looked at the Thai.

'Mr Morgan's right,' he agreed briskly. 'We're only going round in circles.'

'I only wish to establish the facts for myself,' the deputy said cautiously. 'You realise many other companies are bidding?'

'You won't get a better offer than ours,' Kane asserted, tapping his fingers impatiently on the teak desk. 'And more to the point, we're honest and have enormous experience. Look at our record and see for yourself. There's no point constructing a highway that'll crack up in five years.'

'I appreciate that,' the man said. 'But——'

'We're the best people in the business.' Kane cut across him, and snapping his brief case shut, bade the man a tense 'good night', and walked out.

Mark Victorsen, several years older and half a head shorter than his employer, caught up with him halfway down the corridor. 'Bit abrupt, weren't you?'

'Not as abrupt as I'd like to have been. The man's a pedantic fool! If I'd let him drone on, we'd have been there for the night.'

'Which would hardly have endeared me to my wife,' Mark murmured. 'I promised her this would be a second honeymoon!'

Kane chuckled. 'How's Angela enjoying Thailand?'

'Very much. But Terry's bored with hotel life.'

'Terry? Oh yes! I'd forgotten you brought him with you.'

'That's what Angela says too!' came the reply. 'He

hasn't any kids to play with here, and he's running a bit wild.'

'How old is he now?'

'Eight.'

Kane pulled a face. 'I haven't seen him since he was five. Remiss of me.'

'In more ways than one,' the older man said with the ease of a long standing and trusted associate. 'You work yourself too hard, Kane. The only time you relax is the exact second you put your signature on a contract! Then a second later your mind's on the next deal!'

'I relax on other occasions too,' came the dry rejoinder. 'I'm not a monk!'

'Oh that!' Mark was dismissive. 'You need a proper relationship with a woman. Something lasting as well as exciting. Hasn't "off with the old and on with the new" become a mite boring after all these years?'

About to utter a decisive 'no', Kane hesitated and reflected on the question. 'Well, yes, now you mention it. But I figured it was because I was getting old!'

'Rubbish! You're just getting bored with the continuing chase and the same old routine. Find yourself *one* woman—the right one, of course—and watch your libido return!'

'Where do I find the right one?' Kane demanded. 'And how will I know when I have?'

'There speaks a cynic!' Mark Victorsen shook his head. 'Once you've made up your mind you want to get married, you'll soon find what you're looking for. But as long as you're running scared, you never will.'

'I'm not scared, Mark. Simply cautious about committing myself.'

They reached the vestibule and climbed into their waiting car.

'Do you think we'll get the contract?' Victorsen asked as they swung into the main road.

'We've got the best chance. That new concrete mix of ours has enabled us to come in at an incredibly low price. And incidentally, if we do get the job, I'll want you here to keep costs down. You're the best man I have.'

'Nice of you to say so.'

'I'm not being nice. Simply factual. I'd soon tell you if I thought you couldn't do it.'

The older man grinned. 'You're not called "honest Morgan" for nothing!'

'It's the best policy in the end,' Kane said, then added: 'Among men, that is. Women don't see it that way. They prefer you to put on an act. Makes them feel at home, I guess! I've yet to meet a straightforward one.'

'That's because you mix in the wrong circles. Give up the jet set and start dating in the Bromley area!'

Kane laughed. When Mark went off on this tack it was best not to comment. He glanced again at the man who had been his assistant for ten years. He knew little about his personal life, though he had met Angela Victorsen a few times in England, and they had dined together once in Bangkok. She didn't like going with her husband on his foreign trips, which could be a disadvantage if he wanted him in Thailand for a year.

Kane stretched out his legs and stared at the passing traffic. Lord, was it ten years since he had set up on his own? Since he had stormed out of Jack Armitage's office, vowing never to work for a boss again?

'You'll come crawling back,' old Armitage had roared after him. But he never had. Instead he had started his own company, taking Mark with him.

'I can't give you the same salary as Armitage,' he had said at the time, 'but if you stick with me, you'll end up with far more than you'd ever get from that hard-nosed swine!'

'That's my feeling too,' Mark had replied, his confidence in the younger man's ability being justified by subsequent events.

'When do you think we'll hear about our tender?' Mark asked now.

'Your guess is as good as mine. More contractors are arriving next week, as you know, so we'll have to be patient. Right now I'm angling for a meeting with the Prime Minister, but Bonlam's holding me off.'

'Can't Tassy swing it for you?'

'She won't openly defy her father.'

Their car drew up at the hotel and the two men alighted.

'Are you free to have dinner with us tonight?' Mark asked.

'Sorry, but no. I'm dining with Tassy.'

'You're welcome to bring her, though I assume you'd rather be alone?'

'Don't assume anything,' Kane retorted. 'And don't let your imagination run away with you!'

Mark grinned, and followed the younger man to the elevator. They parted company on the fifth floor, and Kane continued to his penthouse suite.

It was a relief to enter the peace of his living room, and he took off his tie and flung his jacket on a chair. How cool it was here compared with the oppressive heat outside. No one could survive in this country without air-conditioning.

Pouring himself a whisky, he flopped into an armchair by the window. He was exhausted to his bones. Jetting to London every other week wasn't conducive to relaxation, and unless he watched himself, he would become depressed and moody; hardly the right frame of mind in which to deal with touchy Ministers. Look how he had lost his cool in the garden yesterday. He had been inexcusably rude to that girl. She was attractive, too, he mused, and he had liked her bluntness—in retrospect! Tassy wouldn't have reacted like that. Come to think of it, he didn't know *how* she'd have behaved. Even after two months she was an enigma. But an extremely seductive one. Finishing his drink, he rose reluctantly to his feet. A shower would revive him and put him in the mood for an evening out with her.

Stripping off his clothes, he stepped under the water. He kept it cool, but after he had soaped himself, he let it run cold. It tingled his skin and he began to feel refreshed and ready for anything. Turning off the taps, he dried himself, then in the nude, ran an electric shaver over his chin. Women found his dark looks attractive—no point denying it—but it necessitated a twice daily shave when he was going out at night. Damn bore it was! He rubbed his fingers along his cheeks; they were smooth enough for Tassy not to complain. If things went well tonight, he might drop her another hint about meeting the Prime Minister. He grinned as he went into the bedroom and started to dress. What a devious bastard I am, he thought, and consoled himself with the fact that if he got this contract, he would be helping British exports.

The telephone rang, and he answered it.

It was Tassy, charmingly extricating herself from their date.

'My father's been asked to dine with the Japanese Ambassador,' she explained, in her soft, melodious voice, 'and he wants me to join them.'

'It's a pretty sudden invitation, isn't it?' he commented. 'Normally these things are planned well in advance.'

'Do you think I'm making it up?' Tassy asked. 'Don't you know I'd rather be with you?'

'If you say so.'

'I do,' she breathed huskily. 'Please forgive me for standing you up.'

'I'll forgive you anything—almost,' he said. 'I've stood people up myself, because of business!'

She laughed. 'A touch of your own medicine, eh?'

'Yes. And I don't like it!'

'Poor Kane.' Still laughing, she put down the telephone.

Slowly he did the same. He had not been joking when he said he didn't like it, for though her excuse seemed genuine enough, he was put out that she had not let him know earlier. Catching sight of himself in the mirror that lined the wall behind his king size bed, he frowned at himself. Only his ego was dented; his genuine feelings were untouched. The knowledge disturbed him, for it implied Tassy meant less to him than he had thought. Either that, or he was getting old! Yet the swift arousal of his body whenever he was near her assured him he wasn't quite a geriatric.

Moving closer to the mirror, he studied himself. The intensity of his expression made him seem older than his thirty-three years, though his body was that of a twenty-year-old. Well, perhaps a little more mature, but definitely lithe and fit, with the perfect co-ordination of well-attuned muscles. Maybe he should do as Mark had suggested and marry. Trouble was he hadn't met the girl with whom he would want to spend the rest of his life, and he had no intention of settling for second best. He would rather remain a bachelor.

Still, even if he found someone he thought perfect, there was no guarantee they'd be happy. Marriage was a gamble whichever way one looked at it. His cynical friends kept telling him so! Only Mark was the exception. He had been married for sixteen years and had been over the moon when his son was born eight years ago. It really was ages since he had seen the child, but he remembered him as a cute little chap. No wonder Mark hated being away from home.

Kane strolled into the dressing room and surveyed his clothes: rows of lightweight suits, and shelves full of pure silk shirts and finest cotton underwear; the bonus that came with being rich. He reached for a grey suit, then paused. He wasn't seeing Tassy, so there was no need to be formal. Donning white linen slacks and a black button-up shirt, he decided to eat out anyway.

The loneliness of the ambitious businessman—not only the long distance runner!—hit him at times like this. Travelling the world and staying in luxury hotels was fine, but how much nicer if he had a wife in England to return to, or better still, one to share his travels until children came along. When they did, he'd leave most of the travelling to his executives; he had no intention of being a part-time parent. His own father, a British army officer, had sent him to boarding school when he was seven, and he had seen his parents only once a year, when he had flown out to join them for the summer vacation, first in Cyprus and later in Hong Kong.

What sort of wife did he want? Kane asked himself as he rubbed Givenchy after-shave on his face. She'd have to like children and be an excellent hostess, that went without saying. She would also have to be intelligent, elegant, and charming. Every virtue and no vice, he thought, grinning at his reflection, and knew he was looking for the impossible. Small wonder he was still single! One day he would have to make up his mind to settle for less. But should it be a homebody who had nothing more on her mind than clothes, kids and cooking, or a career girl who'd keep him mentally on his toes? If truth be told, he wanted both, and he doubted he would find it.

Tassy came closer to fitting the bill than anyone, except that he didn't feel completely at home with her. Maybe it was their different cultural backgrounds, or the fact that he wasn't in love with her. Yet he was daily growing fonder, and who knew what their relationship would be by the time he left Thailand?

In a better frame of mind, he left the hotel and strolled towards Patpong, the centre of Bangkok's night life. It reminded him of Soho, with its blaze of flashing neon lights and jam-packed crowds and traffic. After wandering idly for a while, he paused at the kerb to cross the road and look at the myriad restaurants jostling one upon the other, many interspersed by drinking bars filled with young girls plying their charms. But there was no break in the stream of vehicles thundering past, and he decided to stay on the same side until he found some traffic lights. As he turned to walk again, he bumped into a woman coming from the opposite direction.

'Oops!' He put out his hand to steady her, then saw it was the blonde he had already tangled with twice. Definitely not his day!

She recognised him at the same time, and backed away as if from a snake. It was a gesture that hurt his pride, and he tightened his hold on her.

'Anything wrong?' he asked.

'No. I'm just trying to get a taxi, but they're all full.'

'Are you going back to the hotel?'

She looked mutinous, as if unwilling to reply, then thought better of it and nodded. 'Yes. I was going to a restaurant, but I don't like the look of any of the places around here.'

'I'm not surprised. You're in the red light district!'

'Oh!' She went scarlet, then looked at him with such a strange expression that he burst out laughing.

'No, no, that is *not* how I find my companionship! I was merely strolling along—as you were—looking for a taxi. And I suggest you wait with me.'

'No thanks.'

She turned away, and irritably he called after her. 'You're a brave woman to wander around Bangkok on your own. Particularly in this district.'

'I'm as safe here, as with you!'

'I doubt that. Are you still annoyed with me, Miss—I'm afraid I don't know your name.'

'Sharon Kingston. And I'm not annoyed with you, Mr Morgan. You are entitled to your opinions and——'

'I didn't mean everything I said,' he interrupted her. 'I was goading you on half the time. And you rose so beautifully to the bait, that it made me worse.'

'You meant quite a few of the things you said, though.' She was not to be mollified easily.

'That you're beautiful, yes. And that I fancied you. But I do take no for an answer, and I don't try to bed *all* the desirable females I meet!'

With a shrug she walked away, and he watched her, still piqued by her refusal to share a taxi with him. Without knowing why, he followed her, keeping a safe distance so she remained unaware of it. At the junction of Patpong and Suriwong Road she stopped, obviously not knowing which way to go.

'Excuse me,' he heard her ask a passing couple, before the traffic drowned the rest of her words.

But they could not help her, for she saw them shake their heads and smile—indicating they were strangers too—and she walked on again. There was a decidedly dejected droop to her shoulders, and he quickened his pace, reaching her as she unsuccessfully hailed a taxi.

'Sure you won't let me take you back to the hotel?' he asked, keeping all amusement from his voice.

'Yes—no! I'm fine.' She was preparing to hurry away when she noticed two young men eyeing her from a shop doorway. One of them took a step in her direction and she panicked. 'I think I'll accept your offer after all.'

'You mean better the devil you know?'

'Something like that,' she said coolly.

His amusement grew. She still had her hackles up, and he would enjoy clipping them for her!

'Sure I can't persuade you to have dinner with me?' he murmured. 'After all, I'm a guest at your hotel, and in the interest of business alone . . .'

'That's blackmail, Mr Morgan.'

'You're quite right, Miss Kingston, and I take it back. You are not obliged to accept my invitation. I simply hoped you would.'

'Why?' Her gaze was frank. 'I've been very rude to you.'

'As I was to you. That's why I was hoping we could declare a truce.'

Put like that, he knew she could not refuse without appearing ungracious.

'Very well, Mr Morgan,' she said stiltedly. 'I *will* have dinner with you.'

'Great.' He had finally won, and was pleased with himself. Dining with a pretty girl—even one he did not know—was better than dining alone!

CHAPTER FIVE

THEY walked for several minutes in silence, until a faint gasp made him stop. Glancing at her he saw she was panting.

'Anything wrong, Miss Kingston?'

'Nothing. But—er—do you always walk as if you're in a marathon?'

'Sorry! You should have asked me to slow down.' His eyes went to her feet. 'Tell me, why do you wear such high heels?'

'Because they're flattering.'

Her honesty amused him. 'Your legs don't need flattering. They'd look good even in slippers.'

'The floppy ones with fur inside?' she asked.

'Especially if they have pink bobbles on the front!'

For the first time she laughed, and he was surprised how radiant it made her face.

'How long have you been at the hotel?' he enquired casually.

'A month. And I'll be here another five.'

'What's your job?'

'In the main I take care of our package tour guests.'

'Sounds interesting.' It didn't, but he wasn't anxious to deflate her. However, her next words surprised him, as did the sardonic look which accompanied them.

'You don't mean that, Mr Morgan. To you, my job sounds the most boring in the world.'

'Well . . .'

'But it isn't. It's frustrating, irritating, and sometimes I could take a few heads and bang 'em together—but boring it never is!'

'Point taken,' he said. 'And I wasn't talking down to you, if that's what you think. I was simply trying to be polite.'

'Then there's a first time for everything!'

He laughed. This girl was sharp. Surprisingly so.

'Do you do the same work in England?' he asked.

'Almost. But I'll be changing jobs when I go back. I'm hoping to be given a small hotel to manage.'

'Are you, indeed? Then you really are a full-blown career girl!'

'You object to them?'

'Not at all.' He saw she was on the defensive. 'Every woman has a right to do what she most enjoys.'

'Providing she doesn't encroach on male territory, you mean?'

'Don't put words into my mouth, Miss Kingston. If a competent woman engineer applied for a job in my company, her application would be given the same consideration as a man's.'

'How many woman engineers do you employ?'

'None.'

'Then you——'

'Because none have applied,' he cut across her, and before she could answer, flagged down a cruising taxi and bundled her in.

'Obee Restaurant,' he ordered the driver, as he got in beside her. 'I think you need a good meal,' he added. 'It'll save you taking a bite out of me!'

As the taxi made its way to one of the best restaurants in Bangkok, Kane suddenly regretted asking this girl to dine with him. Thinking about it, he did not relish the prospect of spending an evening making idle talk with someone he didn't know, and he couldn't think why he had let himself in for it. Maybe he was tired of his own company, or Tassy had upset him more than he cared to admit? Still, the invitation

had been proferred and accepted, and he had to make
the best of it.

They drew up outside a palatial, glass-fronted
restaurant and the girl seemed to shrink back in her
seat.

'Perhaps I'll—I think I'll keep on the taxi if you
don't mind, and go back to the hotel.'

'Why?' He was surprised.

'Because I'm not dressed for a place like this.'

'Nonsense.' Her insistence that they part annoyed
him. He should be the one to say he'd rather eat alone,
not the other way around! 'You look fine to me,' he
asserted. 'No one dresses up in Bangkok anyway.'

'That's not true.'

'What I meant was that dressing up is optional.
Anyway, you look lovely.'

He gave her another, closer inspection, approving
both the aquamarine colour of her dress, and its style:
full-skirted and not too tight on top, though it still
showed she had a good figure. Stunning, come to
think of it. Tiny waist, nicely rounded hips and full
breasts. His eyes lingered on them. Full yet firm, their
swell visible even above the conservative neckline.

Reassured by his comment, she let him escort her
into the restaurant, and over to the side of the foyer.

'Shoes off,' he commanded.

'What?'

'Shoes, not clothes!' he grinned. 'It's the custom
to remove your shoes in a restaurant. It makes it
easier to sit cross-legged on the floor—which we'll
be doing.'

He discarded his own and left them on the floor
beside dozens of others, then watched as she stepped
out of her high-heeled sandals. Lovely legs too, he
noted, and they seemed to go on forever. She was
taller than average yet didn't give that impression,

probably because she was so beautifully proportioned.
Once more his eyes roved over her, and aware of it,
she gave him a haughty stare. Serve him right, he
thought amusedly, she wasn't a piece of merchandise
to be examined before buying, and he had no business
eyeing her as if she were.

Shoeless, they followed the waiter into the dining
room—a softly lit room with walls draped in golden
silk, the floor covered with a deeper gold and scarlet
carpet, except for the centre which was bare and
highly polished. They were shown to a low table—not
more than two feet off the ground—and seated on
plump cushions.

'They obviously don't believe in lounging back
while you're eating,' she joked.

'You'll be surprised how comfortable it is,' Kane
told her. 'It just takes a bit of getting used to.'

'But easier if you have short legs!'

'You can say that again!' He crossed his long ones
and leaned an elbow on the table. 'It's a set menu
here, by the way. Thai food only, but they've toned it
down for Western palates.'

'Toned it down?'

'Otherwise it would burn off the roof of your
mouth. Now it only singes it!'

'Oh, great!'

'Trust me,' he smiled. 'You'll like it. Now what'll
you have to drink? Wine doesn't go with this sort of
food, though I can recommend whisky.'

'Well . . .'

'Trust me some more and say yes.'

'Yes, then!' Her head tilted. 'You're very sure of
yourself.'

'Part of my success.'

'In business, you mean?'

'With women too. Sorry! That makes me sound

bloody conceited. What I meant was that most women prefer decisive men.'

She did not answer, and he applauded her silence.

'We'll be seeing some Thai dancing later on,' he added. 'Seen any before?'

'Yes, of course. At the hotel.'

'You'll find it considerably better here. They pay their girls a fortune.'

'So they should,' she replied. 'They have to study for years, and their life as a dancer doesn't go on for long.'

'You sound knowledgeable about it.'

'Guide books,' she confessed. 'I read as much about Thailand as I could, though I must have skipped the bit about taking off your shoes in a restaurant.'

'Not all restaurants,' he corrected. 'Many of them are Westernised now.'

'That's a pity.'

He nodded and beckoned a waiter over to say they were ready to eat.

Their drinks came with their soup—a sour one flavoured with lemon grass—and she seemed to enjoy both. Then came bowls of rice, cooked local fashion without salt, and served with chicken curry and side-dishes of sliced bananas, chutney, chopped water chestnuts, hard-boiled eggs, cucumber relish and crisp fried onions.

She tucked into everything, and Kane enjoyed watching her. It was good to see someone eat with enjoyment, instead of picking at her food as so many of his girlfriends did. They ate silently for a while, and he was glad she did not make pointless conversation when she had nothing particular to say. It was a change from the constant yackity-yak he had become accustomed to hearing.

'Do you know Thailand well, Mr Morgan?' she asked suddenly.

'Kane please, and you are . . .?'

'Sharon.'

'Yes. I know the country quite well. It's a promisng market for my kind of business. The Thais need more roads, hospitals, bridges. The King likes a mix-and-match of Eastern and Western. He was born in America, you know.'

'Have you met him?'

'At official receptions only.'

'I find Thai people difficult to know,' she said. 'They're always polite and charming, but I feel they put up a barrier you can never cross.'

'I know what you mean. I guess the gap between West and East precludes complete intimacy.' As he said it, he thought of Tassy, and wondered if he should amend his remark, then decided against it, and concentrated on his companion. 'Would you like a sweet? If you haven't yet tried a Sonkaya, I suggest you do. It's made from coconut milk and tastes like crème caramel.'

'Sounds wonderful,' Sharon said, 'but I'm not sure if I have any room. I've made a real pig of myself.'

She nibbled on her lower lip and he noticed how white and even her teeth were. In the pink glow of the room her skin was radiant and her hair shone like spun gold. She was remarkably pretty—no, beautiful, come to think of it, with large blue eyes and preposterously long lashes. False? He leaned closer. No, they were real enough. He looked at her mouth, with its short upper lip and fuller lower one, hinting at sensuousness, and unexpectedly longed to kiss it. Yet her total impression was of virginal innocence—probably because of her frank, unflinching gaze. Yet she couldn't be *that* innocent. Few girls were these days.

He was still staring at her when the lights dimmed, and she turned to the stage. This gave him a view of her profile, which was even more disarmingly young, and he felt a pang of annoyance with himself.

I'm cradle-snatching, he thought, and tried to appease his conscience by telling himself he had rescued her from a melancholy evening alone—as she had rescued him. He was doing nothing more wicked than buying her dinner. He had no intention of seducing her.

An attractive Thai girl, in a red-and-blue brocade panung and long-sleeved jacket, came on stage and explained in French and English the story of the dance they were about to perform. Then to the accompaniment of gongs, drums and cymbals, the dancers appeared and began their intricate and delicate movements, twisting their bodies with graceful yet erotic gestures. They wore richly coloured long silk dresses sparkling with jewels, and tall gold head-dresses, and their hands, malleable as putty, seemed extraordinarily long because of the fantastic length of their finger nails.

'How did you like it?' Kane asked Sharon as the dance ended to wild applause.

'Very much.' Her eyes were glowing with pleasure. 'I agree with you that it's better than in our hotel. There's no comparison. It's so much more authentic here, though I couldn't follow the story.'

'I'm not surprised,' he said with amusement. 'The gestures have hidden religious meanings—as well as sexual ones.'

'Even I could see *that*!'

'Why "even you"?' he asked, and saw the colour bloom in her cheeks.

She did not reply, and he knew his first impression of her had been correct.

'An innocent,' he murmured. 'That's extremely rare these days—especially among career girls.'

She looked at him in sudden anger, then unexpectedly started to laugh. 'How old-fashioned you are! Do you think women only succeed via the bed—from bedroom to boardroom?'

'Not *my* boardroom,' he retorted. 'The prettier the female, the harder they'd find it to get *anywhere* in my organisation.'

'That's equally biased! I hope you don't mean it?'

'I certainly do. Pretty women use their sex appeal to get what they want, and most men fall over themselves to help them! But a plain lady knows she has to rely on her ability—hence she works twice as hard to succeed.'

Kane paused, aware of—and enjoying—the fury in the bright blue eyes opposite him. He waited for her outburst, and was not disappointed.

'So I take it you make sure your female employees are plain Janes?'

'Not at all. Let's say I prefer them to be. But as I mentioned to you earier, our staff are chosen on merit.'

'I suppose it doesn't matter how handsome your male employees are?' she asked sarcastically.

'You're dead right. In the office or on the factory floor, Adonis gets the same treatment as Caliban!' Kane paused then said mischievously: 'Of course things may change once we start having forewomen!'

'I doubt it,' Sharon sniffed. 'Women aren't as susceptible to looks as men!'

'Aha! So you agree in parts with what I say. In general, men *are* pushovers when it comes to sex, and women use it to their advantage.' He paused, waiting for her to fly at him.

Golden hair glinted in the lamp glow as she shook her head. 'I've no desire to argue with you again, Mr Mor—Kane,' she amended.

'You mean you're giving in?'

'I mean you're too clever with words!'

'Especially when they happen to be true!' he chuckled. 'You're very young, Sharon, but given maturity, you'll come round to my way of thinking.'

'You mean when I'm too old to use my looks to achieve success?' she enquired with heavy sarcasm.

'I mean when you're old enough to look back and see the progress of your career. *You* will succeed because you're clever as well as beautiful. It's not an idle compliment; I mean it. But when you're older and wiser, you'll admit that your looks were a help, not a hindrance.'

'I'll admit that right now! Of course looks count. I'd be a fool if I didn't realise it. All I'm saying is that most women don't deliberately use their looks to disarm the men they work with.'

'We'd better agree to differ on that, before we come to blows.'

She sniffed. 'You're talking down to me, Kane. I'm not inexperienced in commercial life, you know. I have six years' hotel management behind me, working with men and women equally.'

'Six years? You don't look a day over twenty.'

'I'm twenty-four.'

Not quite as young as he had thought. So he wasn't cradle-snatching after all. Just toddler-snatching! The waiter hovered beside him and he ordered coffee.

'I believe it's a difficult training,' he went on. 'You have to go through the whole spectrum of hotel work, don't you, from chambermaiding to waiting at table?'

'Yes. How come you're so knowledgeable? As far as I'm aware, there aren't any books on the subject!'

He laughed. 'Put it down to natural curiosity. A friend of mine runs a hotel, and I've asked him about it. I'm interested in people.'

'Yet you don't deal with people. You construct *things*.'

He did not hide his amusement. 'Nevertheless it's my ability to relate to others that enables me to get the *orders* to construct things. Also, people use what we build, and it's important to consider their needs. I owe my success to that premise.'

'It's a noteworthy success.'

'Now you're flattering me.'

'It was genuinely meant. Not as a "thank you" for my supper!'

'Sheath your claws, Sharon, I believe you.' He sipped his coffee. 'But let's talk some more about you. Is hotel management going to be your entire life, or will you use your training to run an efficient home for some lucky man?'

'Both,' she said seriously. 'I'd like to go on working after I'm married.'

'Most women only do so for financial reasons.'

'At the moment, yes. But more and more want outside stimulus—something to relieve the tedium of housework and looking after children.' She hestitated, then said: 'If you—when *you* get married, would you object to *your* wife wanting a career?'

'Not unless she objected to mine! But seriously, what right would I have to stop her? I regard marriage as a total partnership, with both partners getting what they want from it. That's Utopian thinking, of course. Generally one or other of them has to compromise.'

'It's usually the woman!'

'I won't argue there.'

'That's a relief!'

Chuckling, he paid the bill and they left the restaurant. The evening had turned out to be far more stimulating than he had envisaged, and he was reluctant to end it.

'Shall we go on somewhere to dance? I know a nice place down by the river.'

'I'd like that,' she said.

A cab took them through Patpong—still ablaze with garish lights—to a disco near their hotel. Air-conditioned and softly lit, with music playing the latest hits, it could have been anywhere in the world.

Sharon surprised him by being an excellent dancer with a marvellous sense of rhythm. She was pliant and fluid, and the feel of her in his arms aroused him in a way he hadn't anticipated. Normally he made it a rule to steer clear of girls who didn't know the score, not because he didn't like innocence, but because it could lead to complications, to promises made that he had no intention of keeping. One day he might be ready for a commitment, so he told himself, but the future was always ahead. Yet somehow tonight he found himself giving it thought, and wondered anew whether he shouldn't stop playing the field and settle down.

'May we sit out the next dance, Kane? I'm breathless.'

Sharon's request brought him back to the immediate present, and he led her back to their table. His hands still wanted to touch her and his thighs stirred at the thought of pressing himself against the curves of her body, feeling her beautiful breasts swell beneath his fingers, her mouth open to his. God! he wanted her.

'Is it possible to get a cold drink?' she asked. 'Something long and non-alcoholic?'

'No problem.' As he concentrated on her request, his self-control reasserted itself, and he determined to keep it that way.

'You should try to see something of the country while you're here,' he said flatly. 'It's a fascinating mixture of old and new. In Bangkok you could almost be in London, but in the country you would feel in a different century.'

'That's what everyone says. But I doubt if I'll have much time to go far afield.' She looked rueful. 'On my next day off I'm going to visit some of the temples and the Floating Market.'

'I'll take you, if you like,' he heard himself say. He must be mad! But it was too late to retract. 'Let me know when you're free.'

'You mean you have free time to spare?' she teased.

'At the moment. And it might be a long drawn out one. You see I'm waiting for the Minister's decision.'

'You must find that nerve-racking?'

'I'm used to it. You know the old saying: if you can't stand the heat in the kitchen, don't be a cook!'

'Sometimes one doesn't realise that until it's too late, and by then you've too many commitments to walk out.'

'True.' He leaned towards her. 'You're a perceptive young woman.'

'You mean not just dumb and beauti——' She stopped, embarrassed.

'Not just dumb and beautiful,' he concluded for her. 'Why be afraid to say it? You *are* beautiful. You know that?'

She shrugged. 'Tell me how you started your career.'

'Are you changing the subject?'

'Yes.' Her colour was high but she met his gaze. 'It's safer that way.'

'You want to be safe?' he asked, annoyed to find his voice had grown husky.

'Yes!'

Knowing she was right, and that he'd think the same himself after a cold shower, he shrugged and answered her question.

'I took an engineering degree at Cambridge and

then worked for a construction company in Glasgow, before setting up on my own.'

'Glasgow? You're a Scot?'

'No.' He was sorry to disappoint her. 'It was merely the best job I could get at the time.'

'And when you set up your own company, how long did it take you to become successful?'

'I was successful right away! I'm not boasting, just being honest. But it took a while longer before my company was rich and successful. Now we're one of the biggest and best in the world.'

'And you're one of the youngest tycoons,' she teased.

'Does that turn you on?' he asked bluntly, and regretted his question the instant he saw the red tide of colour flame her face. 'Sorry,' he said abruptly. 'It was a damned offensive question.'

'I can understand why you asked it, though. You probably get your fill of tycoon crazy groupies!'

She had regained her composure fast, and he silently applauded her for it. 'More than my fill,' he said aloud. 'I'm astonished how many women are "turned on" by a man who has power or fame or money. They enjoy the thrill of basking in his reflected glory.'

'And when one has all three—plus being handsome,' she added, 'I bet the ladies are three deep!'

He laughed outright. 'You think I'm conceited, eh?'

'No. Simply a realist!'

'I'll concede that. I know myself—I hope—and I like to think I know others.' He saw her stifle a yawn, and glancing at his watch was astonished to find it was after one.

'Tired girls should be in bed,' he smiled. 'And I've kept you away from yours too long.'

'My day does start rather early,' she confessed. 'I

like to be downstairs when the big groups go off on a
tour—which always seems to be at the crack of dawn.'

Within minutes they had left the air-cooled disco for
the muggy warmth of the outside, and were soon in a
taxi, speeding back to the Avonmore.

'I've enjoyed myself very much,' Kane said. 'You're
easy to talk to, Sharon.'

'So are you.'

He leaned towards her and she drew back into the
corner of her seat. Clearly, she did not want to kiss
him, and he straightened. But the desire to touch her
was still strong, and he dug his hands into the pockets
of his jacket.

'The child who overturned your table in the garden
was Terry Victorsen,' she said suddenly. 'I thought
you'd like to know.'

For an instant, he did not follow. 'Mark's son?
Good Lord!'

'He didn't know *you* either,' Sharon smiled. 'Or
he'd have been more scared!'

'I doubt if anything would scare that brat!' Kane
said wryly. 'I must make a point of meeting him again.
But to be honest, I tend to keep my head down when I
work.'

'I know,' she said. 'You've passed me a dozen times
in the lobby, yet you only *saw* me in the garden.'

'Which was *my* loss,' he replied swiftly. 'I was
vaguely aware of an attractive blonde at Reception,
but I was too preoccupied to do anything about it.'

'But tonight you took pity on me and——'

'*You* took pity on me,' he corrected. 'It was——' He
stopped as the taxi drew up outside the hotel. Good
thing too, or he would have said more than he
intended. There was something about this girl that got
to him. She was a good looker, of course, but he
wasn't short of beautiful girls. Maybe he was fed up

being away from England, and her cool, blonde looks had got to him. Whatever, he'd better watch his step.

They crossed the foyer together. Despite the hour, Sharon still looked as fresh as a daisy. No, daisy was the wrong description. They were insignificant little flowers, and she resembled something more exotic. Yet cool with it. A white orchid with gold-tipped petals. Yes, that described her exactly.

He paused by the elevator. 'Care for a nightcap?'

'No, thank you.'

Her tone was so prim, he chuckled. 'I wasn't planning on showing you the view from my penthouse! We can have a drink down here.'

'It's still no, I'm afraid. I really am tired.' She put out her hand to say goodnight, but he ignored it and followed her into the elevator.

He said nothing until it stopped at the tenth floor for her, and as he went to get out, she shook her head.

'There's no need to see me to my door, Kane. I'm fine. And thank you for a lovely evening.'

'It was my pleasure,' he said, resolutely keeping his hands in his pockets. 'Be seeing you.'

But letting himself into his suite a few moments later, he wondered if he should. Some evenings were best left as pleasant 'one-off' memories. Trying to repeat them could be a mistake. Yet he could not imagine this being the case with Sharon. Rather the opposite. She had hidden depths that might make her more, not less, interesting.

And that's what bothered him.

CHAPTER SIX

KANE figured in Sharon's dreams that night, and it infuriated her. What was so great about him, anyway? She had known many men equally attractive, intelligent and charming, though she had to admit none had combined all these attributes in such generous proportions!

She sighed and got out of bed. Maybe she was imagining he was all these wonderful things because she was on the rebound from Pete and felt vulnerable and lonely in this foreign city; ready to latch on to the first attractive man who showed even a modicum of interest in her. But it was more than that. Kane had incredible charm and she would be a fool not to admit it, and an even bigger fool if she read more into his friendship than he meant.

In the first instance, Tassy Bonlam was a formidable rival. Sharon pulled herself up sharply. Rival? She was crazy to think such a thing! It presupposed Kane was interested in her, which he wasn't. All he had said was that he found her company pleasant and liked her. She was surprised he hadn't added 'like a sister'.

Trouble was, the storm he aroused in her was far from sisterly, and she was disconcerted that her feelings for Pete had proved so fickle. She puzzled over it, wondering what would have happened if he hadn't been posted abroad. Would their relationship have grown—despite his attitude to working wives—or would she have realised her own feelings weren't deep enough to be sustained over a lifetime?

It was a question she could never answer, and she pushed it from her mind and concentrated on Kane; on his courtesy and deference, his ability to make her feel she was the only woman in the world. Was it genuine or an act? The fact that he was still unmarried presupposed the latter, emphasising her belief that it was dangerous to become involved with him. Yet she was on tenterhooks all day, alternately wanting him to call, and hoping he wouldn't, and being stupidly upset when he didn't!

It was not until the following afternoon, while showing a group of tourists to their rooms in the annexes, that she spotted him and Tassy together under a sun umbrella by the swimming pool. The sight of them lying so intimately close to one another filled her with jealousy, even though she knew she had no justification for it. She was sure she wasn't the only girl he took out to dinner and charmed! She was still brooding over this during her solitary meal later that evening, when she saw him strolling towards her.

'I called your room,' he said, pausing by her table. 'I was hoping you'd have dinner with me.'

Sharon gave him a cool smile. He didn't believe in giving a girl much notice, she thought sourly, and remembering the scene at the poolside, wondered if he had been stood up by the lovely Tassy.

'I was supposed to be dining with Mark Victorsen and his wife,' Kane added, almost as if he guessed her thoughts, 'but their son has a slight fever and they didn't want to leave him.'

'I see.'

He pulled out a chair. 'May I?'

'This table's reserved for the staff.'

'Then come and sit at mine.'

'I'm in the middle of my meal.'

'So what? The waiter can bring it over.' Blue eyes

glinted at her. 'Not ashamed of being seen with me, are you?'

'You must be joking,' she mocked. 'What girl wouldn't give her eye teeth to be seen with the famous Kane Morgan?'

'Such flattery! You expect me to swallow it?'

'Some men will swallow anything!'

'Right now I'll settle for a good claret! Come on, Sharon, say you'll join me.'

Knowing that if she didn't, it would be an admission of hurt pride, she followed him to a table overlooking the garden.

'You have a pretty poor opinion of men,' Kane said when, his order given and the wine served, he raised his glass to her. 'Let's drink a toast to your better understanding of male attitudes!'

Silently she drank, and the glint in his eyes grew more pronounced as she let his toast go unanswered.

'You think that's impossible?' he asked.

'A better understanding of men won't make me change my mind about them,' she replied. 'Most of them are like little boys.'

'Children can be lovable, though!'

'They can also be spoilt and self-centred!'

Kane leaned across the table, the humour in his face gone. 'Sounds as if someone has hurt you pretty badly.'

She hesitated, then nodded. 'Yes.'

'He loved you and left you?'

'Let's just say he left,' she said flippantly. 'Anyway, we weren't suited. He was your typical "macho" male; wouldn't tolerate his wife working—*if* and when he decided to marry.'

'Well at least he made his attitudes clear, so that's something in his favour! Mind you, as I said last night, marriage is generally a question of compromise.

Every partnership is in fact, which is why I've always gone solo. I prefer to run my business *my* way.'

'And your personal life too?'

'I'll take a rain check on that question. Ask me a year from now.'

She almost said he wouldn't remember her by then, but thought it might look as if she were fishing for a compliment. He'd give it, she was sure, but it would be meaningless.

'How's the "big deal" coming along?' she asked, to change the subject.

'Very slowly. A Japanese contingent's coming over to make a bid, so the project's by no means cut and dried.'

He paused as Sharon's entrée was served, then his own, and she saw he had skipped a fish course in order to catch up with her.

'Do you think the Minister's being difficult?' she asked, determined to keep the conversation on a business level.

'Well, there's something going on, that's for sure,' he admitted. 'Tassy said her father thinks that any company who wishes to quote, should be given a chance to do so.'

'That means you could be here for months!' Perhaps even for the duration of her own stay, she thought, and shivered with pleasure and apprehension.

'I've no intention of hanging around for a decision,' he said, sending her hopes crashin. 'I'll give it another month and then pull out. By that time I should know what I'm up against.'

'Price, you mean?'

'And a few other things.'

'Like bribery?'

'Could be.'

He did not elaborate and she concentrated on her food.

'What I'm telling you is confidential,' he said suddenly.

'I realise that,' Sharon looked up. 'But aren't you taking a chance? After all, you barely know me.'

'One can know a person instantly,' he said quietly. 'And some you can "know" for years and still find them incomprehensible. But you're like spring water, Sharon—clear for all to see.'

How dull, she thought, and wished he had likened her to a deep pool, enigmatic and mysterious.

'What's wrong?' he asked. 'Don't you like my compliment?'

'It was a double-edged one.'

'On the contrary. There's nothing more refreshing than spring water.' He motioned the waiter to remove their plates. 'I'll have wasted a helluva lot of time and money if I don't land this contract,' he went on, his comment showing where his real interest lay. 'I'm the only one in my organisation capable of deciding whether or not we stay here and keep pushing for it.'

'You'll always be the only one. You just said you don't like partners!'

'True. But that doesn't mean I don't delegate *some* of my authority.'

'I can't see you delegating much,' she said. 'It's not in your character.'

He made to protest, then shook his head. A lock of hair fell forward and he raked it back impatiently. 'What makes you so sure?'

'Instinct. Anyway, didn't you just say one doesn't need to know a person long, to know them?'

He chuckled. 'I can see I'll have to watch what I say to you. Anyway, whether you believe me or not, I definitely intend easing my workload.'

'When you're seventy?' she teased. 'You've still years of bossing ahead of you!'

'And years of living, as well.' He leaned back in his chair, keeping his eyes on her face. 'You know something? If I died tomorrow, nobody would mourn me.'

The smile left her face and she was genuinely horrified by what he had said.

'I'd be missed,' he went on, 'I grant you that—but only by those dependent on me financially. But cry for me . . .?' He shrugged.

'If you want people to cry for you,' she said quietly, 'you must be willing to cry for them.'

'I did my share when my mother died five years ago. I——' He hesitated. 'I cared for her very much, although as a child we weren't close. It was something we both regretted.'

'Do you have any other family?'

'My father. He was regular army, and now lives in Somerset. I see him every few months, though we've little in common.'

'But surely you have friends?' she asked. 'In your position I'd have thought——'

'Oh, I have plenty of business friends,' he cut in. 'But if my company went bust tomorrow, they'd disappear with it.'

'There's something wrong, somewhere, then. I think——' She stopped, reluctant to be honest. After all, no matter how friendly Kane was being, he was a guest of the hotel, and she an employee.

'Go on,' he urged. 'Out with it. I promise I won't complain to the management!'

Still she hesitated, and his hand came out to clasp hers as it rested on the table. His touch, like the man himself, was firm and cool, and she was intensely aware of the tips of his fingers on her skin.

'Well,' she murmured, withdrawing her hand, 'haven't you ever considered that your lack of close friends could be due to your unwillingness to have any emotional ties? Friendship's a two-way commitment, Kane, and if you want to plough your own furrow, others may see it as your need to be left alone. *You* have to make the first move.'

He twirled the liquid in his glass. It effervesced and bubbles rose to the surface and broke, as illusions frequently did.

'You're right,' he murmured. 'I've know it for a long while but it isn't easy to change. You see, Morgan Construction is not only my work, it's my hobby and I love it.'

'Then don't whinge about having no friends.' The retort came out before she could stop it, and she went scarlet. 'I'm sorry. I'd no right——' Her voice was cut off by his laughter.

'Don't apologise for saying the obvious,' he said when he could speak. 'I've been sitting here full of self-pity and I deserved your reprimand. You're right, my lovely. If I want to change my life, I must change myself.'

'Not too much,' she said quickly. 'You're nice as you are.'

'Watch out!'

'What for?'

'You might begin to like me!'

She already did, and was delighted he didn't know. Deciding she had better bring the subject back to safe ground, she said: 'I hate having to break up this conversation, but I'm due for an early night.'

'Pity. I was hoping we could go on somewhere.'

'I'd fall asleep on you.'

'Is that a promise?'

She felt her face burn and was furious that after all these years she wasn't more sophisticated. 'I've had a busy day, Kane, I'm sorry.'

'Not to worry. There's always another night! But you did promise to let me take you sightseeing,' he added as they left the dining room. 'When are you free?'

Embarrassed, she bit her lip. 'Tomorrow, actually. That's why I want an early night. I'd like to set off before it gets too hot.'

'A good idea. Is eight o'clock too early for you?'

'No, but ... Please, I wasn't fishing for an invitation.'

'I know that. But it will be my pleasure to take you. Unless Bonlam calls me, I'm totally free.'

'If you find you can't make it ...'

'I doubt anything will crop up. And if it does, it might not do Bonlam any harm to find me *not* waiting for his call!'

Kane paused by the elevator, and she tensed, wondering if he was going to suggest seeing her to her room, and not certain what she would say if he did. But even as she considered it, he raised an arm in a laconic wave and turned away.

Was he going to find someone else to share the rest of the evening with him? she asked herself as she prepared for bed. He'd find no shortage of willing girls! He might lack close, personal friends, but he would never lack for women. Like Pete, he had charisma. And like Pete, she reminded herself, he was not for her.

Before dawn, Sharon was awake and sitting on the balcony, sipping fresh papaya juice and watching the mist rise above the golden spires. The drone of traffic, so noticeable during the day, was now only a muted hum, and she could hear the shrill, unfamiliar call of a parakeet, its colourful plumage hidden by the thick glossy leaves of a palm tree.

Kane had not said where they were going, but she assumed it would be the tourist haunts of temples and markets, and after a cool shower she donned a sleeveless white cotton dress, and flat sandals. She kept her hair away from her face with a pearl and tortoiseshell band, and wore the minimum make-up of lip gloss and barrier cream. Thank goodness her eyebrows and lashes were dark. As a child, her friends had teased her about it, for they had looked incongruous with her flaxen hair. But age had turned the flax to burnished gold, and her thick, chestnut brown lashes and curving brows had finally come into their own.

Five minutes before the appointed hour she was waiting in the foyer, dangling a pair of sunglasses from her hand and hoping Kane wouldn't think her too eager.

'There you are!'

She swung round to see him beside her. In jeans and white T-shirt and sandals, he looked carefree as a student, and her heart did a silly flip flop.

'I've brought a scarf,' she said, aware of his intent gaze.

'That'll be too hot. We'll get you a parasol in the market.'

As they stepped outside, a limousine drew up before them and he motioned her to get in. No ordinary taxi for Kane!

'You're looking very beautiful today,' he said as they moved off. 'White suits you.'

'It suits most blondes.'

'Especially real ones!'

She was amused. 'How can you tell I am? My eyebrows and lashes are dark.'

'But your skin isn't. And genuine blonde hair has a special look to it. Like sun on a cornfield.'

She laughed outright. 'Now you're making me feel rustic.'

'Not *you*. You're too imperial looking.

'Really? I don't see myself that way.'

'Well, you are. It's a combination of height and expression. For a tall girl you're singularly graceful.'

Their car swung wide to avoid a wobbling bicycle, and Sharon fell against Kane.

He caught her firmly and held her for an instant. 'Flinging yourself at me, eh?'

'Aren't you used to it?' she joked, to hide her embarrassment.

'Yes,' he said briefly. 'And it gets boring as hell. But most of the girls aren't flinging themselves at *me*— merely at what I represent to them. A fabulous meal ticket.'

'You underestimate yourself, Kane.'

'Thanks.'

She settled back again, this time holding on to the side of the seat, as their driver, with the agility of a porpoise, skimmed past people, rickshaws, bicycles and cars. Every now and then they were caught in a traffic jam, and his horn joined the orchestra of motor hooters. It was a relief when they finally drew to a stop and Kane ushered her out.

They were in front of the Grand Palace, a city within a city on the western side of Bangkok, home of Siamese kings in ancient times. Sharon was enthralled by the slender spires and multi-domed pavilions with the familiar snake-shaped decorations on their roof-tops, which rose behind a high, white-washed wall that seemed to go on for ever.

They walked through a gate flanked by two stone Chinese lions, towards Wat Phra Keo, Temple of the Emerald Buddha. The scene inside the courtyard took her breath away: enchanting gilded fauns, part beast, part human, stood beside demon sentinels twenty-feet tall, holding gigantic swords and wearing crested helmets, while around them was a vast menagerie of stone elephants, cows, bronze lions, painted monkeys, gilded serpents. The morning sun blazed down on the scene, exaggerating the brilliant colours and the motionless air was alive with the soothing tinkle of bells.

Taking off their shoes, they entered the Wat. High above them, on a golden throne, sat the Emerald Buddha; not emerald at all, but green jasper. Groups of worshippers kneeled reverently at its feet, while others placed flowers at the altar or wandered around to gaze at the murals lining the walls, which depicted Lord Buddha's earthly life. And pervading all was the smell of burning incense.

'If you want to go near the Buddha, you have to go on all fours,' Kane whispered, and they both crouched low, allowing the murmur of prayer to surround them.

After several moments, as if by common accord, they simultaneously rose and returned to the court-yard, then ambled through the Palace grounds before crossing the river to see the royal barges, with their dragon prows and gilded figureheads standing high and dry in wooden sheds.

'I'd love to ride in one of them,' Sharon remarked.

'They're only used on ceremonial occasions,' Kane told her. 'Tassy once went in one when an African President was here on a visit.'

Sharon's sense of elation suddenly plummeted as she envisaged the bejewelled Tassy, moving slowly down the river in a royal barge, graciously acknow-ledging the crowds.

'Where to now?' Kane asked, unaware of her thoughts. 'Fancy a stroll back through the Pramane Ground?'

She nodded, and they made their way towards the huge open space in the centre of the city. It was packed with locals and tourists alike, for this was a famous area for kite flying, one of the national pastimes. High above them, in the pale blue sky, flew dozens of star and diamond-shaped kites, many of them in fantastic designs in variegated colours.

'They're having a kite-fighting contest today,' Kane explained. 'That's why I wanted you to see it. Teams of men are flying those heavy ones—they're called chulas, and are supposedly male. The smaller kites are called pakpaos, and are female, and only one person flies it. The idea is for the female pakpao to rise and "flirt" with the chula, and try to bring it down, while the chula counter-attacks and tries to ground the female kite!'

Sharon laughed. 'The battle of the sexes—Thai style! But it's a bit unfair, don't you think?' she asked, as they wended their way through groups of picnickers. 'The chulas are much bigger.'

'Even so, the female kite often wins,' Kane said. 'It's lighter and easier to manipulate. Look—see what I mean? That little purple-and-scarlet one's just grounded that massive brown one.'

'Aren't you glad you're not a kite?' Sharon teased, glancing up at him. The breeze had ruffled his hair and he looked very young striding along with his hands in his pockets.

'I'm too high a flyer to be caught and grounded,' he grinned back, and she noticed the small gap between his two front teeth, which gave him an endearing little-boy look.

'One day someone might wind in your string!' she warned.

'One day I may be ready for it!'

Sharon ignored his answer, yet felt she had to say something. 'Did you enjoy yourself last night?'

'Last night? But I had dinner with *you*.'

'I . . . er . . . I thought you went out afterwards.'

For an instant he looked blank. 'Oh, I took a walk along the river. Very romantic in the moonlight. I'm sorry you weren't with me.'

So was she, she admitted silently, knowing nothing would induce her to say it aloud, and she gave her attention to the numerous stalls lining the edge of the park. Here one could buy anything from live chickens and ducks, to shoes, mousetraps, jeans and dresses, ceremonial swords, and even Siamese cats—though there weren't as many around as she had expected!

'Mustn't forget your parasol,' Kane explained, seeing Sharon shade her face with her hand, and led her to a stall covered with dozens, in every imaginable colour. 'This is you exactly,' he commented, picking up a gold one decorated with bright blue flowers. 'Matches your hair and your eyes!' His own crinkled. 'It'll even do for the monsoon. The paper is oiled to keep out the rain.'

He paid for it and opened it for her. As she took it from him, their fingers touched and she felt a tremor of desire. But his next remark brought her to earth again.

'We'll have to cut today a bit short, I'm afraid. I've a conference at four with Mr Bonlam, and I have to make a few calls to London first.'

'I thought you said you weren't going to make yourself available to him today?'

'I changed my mind. Or rather Mark made me change it. Anyway, maybe we can meet after dinner? I know I'll be free by then. How about making it the American bar at ten?'

'Fine,' she said gaily. She had expected to spend the entire day with Kane, and wondered if his excuse was genuine or if he had invented it to get away. 'I'm tired anyway,' she lied, 'and I'll have a rest and then write home.'

'But you will let me see you later?'

'Do you really want to?' she asked bluntly.

'I rarely say what I don't mean, Sharon. When you know me better, you'll realise it.'

Would she know him better? It was a question that nagged at her for the rest of the day and, despite what he had said, she did not know the answer, and was in two minds whether to accept his invitation.

CHAPTER SEVEN

AT eight that evening she took her usual table in the dining room, where she was joined by Mr Chittiwera, who was on night duty.

'Had a good day?' he asked.

'Lovely, thanks. I went sightseeing this morning.'

'You know you can always go on one of our tours?'

'I—er—I went with Mr Morgan,' she answered briefly, tensing for Mr Chittiwera's comment. But beyond a faint look of surprise, he made none.

'Miss Bonlam was here this morning, asking for him,' he said unexpectedly.

'Does that mean there's more news about the highway contract?' Mr Chittiwera was always a good source of gossip.

'No. Though I'm sure Miss Bonlam knows more than she admits. I hope Mr Morgan realises it.'

'I'd be surprised if he didn't,' Sharon said lightly. 'I bet he knows the score—in every way.'

Reluctant to continue discussing Kane, she unobtrusively changed the subject. Her hesitancy about meeting him in the bar had increased, and after dinner she went for a walk in the garden. Because of what had happened with Pete, her emotions were still too raw for her to court another rebuff, and with all the will in the world she could not imagine any future with a man as dynamic as Kane, who inhabited a world so different from her own. Once he left the Avonmore their paths would never cross. On the other hand, if she bore this in mind and resolved to steer clear of any deep involvement with him, maybe she could enjoy a light-hearted flirtation?

With this in mind, she went into the American bar and found him already there. He had discarded his casual attire for an impeccably cut dark silk suit—probably for dinner with Mr Bonlam—and his hair was carefully smoothed down, though an errant lock threatened to fall over his forehead. He really had no right to be so devastating!

'I missed you,' he said seriously, holding out a chair for her. 'I thought you weren't coming.'

No doubt he had expected to find her waiting for him! She gave him a bright smile.

I was in the garden and forgot the time. How did your conference go?'

'Hard to tell. A lot of promises but all in the air—not on paper! I had a good dinner though. Mrs Bonlam's in Paris, and Tassy was hostess.'

'Does she live with her parents?'

'Sure. This is the Far East, you know. Well-brought-up young women don't do their own thing—at least not openly! The Bonlams have a beautiful home north of the city, and a seaside villa at Pattaya. Now what'll you drink? You aren't going to stick with coffee I hope?'

'A glass of wine, then.'

He murmured something to the hovering waiter, and a few minutes later they were sipping champagne from tall, slim glasses, the dark green bottle in the ice bucket proclaiming it a Krug '73.

'Fabulous,' Sharon said appreciatively. 'But very extravagant.'

'What's money for?' He shrugged. 'Wouldn't *you* spend it if you had it?'

'*Some* of it,' she conceded.

'On clothes and jewellery?'

'A few clothes, yes, but I don't fancy being weighed

down by diamonds!'

'They aren't your stone anyway.' His gaze narrowed on her. 'Sapphires and emeralds are far more you.'

'I'll remember that when I make my first million! Tell me what *your* extravagances are, Kane?'

'Let me get one thing clear first. I believe that if one wants something and can afford it, it isn't an extravagance to buy it. Personally, I have a good wardrobe, which is a business necessity anyway.'

'No cigars or sports cars?'

'I don't smoke, nor am I into cars. To me, they're a necessity. But I do have a jet and a helicopter,' he added, and as she giggled, he realised the humour of what he had said, and laughed. 'They belong to the business, though, so they don't qualify as a personal extravagance. As I said, my lifestyle's modest and I plough my own profits back into the company. I aim to double our assets in the next two years.'

'For the challenge of it, or because you want to leave your children a fortune?'

'I don't believe in too much inherited wealth. Everyone should work for their money, and so will any children of mine.'

'I didn't expect you to say that.'

His eyebrows rose, two silky, dark arcs. 'You mean you've given some thought to me?'

Her colour rose, but her voice remained cool. 'Of course. Good hoteliers should be able to assess their guests.'

'But on your own admission you wrongly assessed *me*!'

'On the personal level only. I still think I can anticipate what you'd require of a hotel.'

'Tell me,' he said silkily.

She looked him straight in the eye. 'First-class

accommodation, peace and quiet to work, and very discreet staff.'

'I'm not certain what you mean by that last remark,' he teased. 'You think I hold orgies?'

'That's not my concern.'

'Pity. I was hoping——' He was interrupted by a waiter coming over to say there was a call for him from England.

'I'll take it in my room.' He rose. 'Sorry about this, Sharon. I'll be quick as I can.'

It was half an hour before he was back, his face flushed, his eyes sparkling.

'I was right to order champagne,' he said. 'A large contract which I thought had fallen through, has just been confirmed. We're to start work right away.'

'In England?'

'Wales, actually. I'm flying home tomorrow.'

To Sharon's relief, Kane turned to signal the waiter for the bill, and did not see her face. The knowledge that he was leaving had hit her with a force she had not anticipated, and it was difficult to hide her feelings. Yet she had to make the effort.

'Does that mean you're giving up on the Thai contract?'

'Lord, no! But Mark's more than capable of controlling the situation here. Anyway, I've little choice. A bird in the hand is worth two in the bush, and I can't wait here for ever.'

'So you're delegating responsibility at last!' she said, forcing a smile.

'This is an exception!'

'And you won't be coming back?'

Kane stared at her as if trying to probe her thoughts. 'Only to sign the contract—if it ever gets to that stage. Otherwise, no.' His eyes were still on her, and a smile slowly curved the corners of his mouth.

'Don't tell me you'll miss me?'

'A little. You're an amusing man.' Smoothing her skirt, she rose. 'Well, have a good journey, Kane.'

'Why are you going to bed so early?'

The question surprised her. 'You just paid the bill and I assumed you had a lot to do.'

'You assumed wrong. I'm just too restless to sit still. I thought we'd have a stroll in the garden. Come on, darling, keep me company.'

She knew the endearment was casually uttered and didn't mean a thing to him, yet it made her foolish heart beat faster as they left the bar and went outside.

It was still warm, and the full moon and chirping crickets lent an intriguing foreignness to the night. A mosquito zoomed down and bit her arm, and she rubbed her skin vigorously.

'One of the benefits of the climate,' Kane said dryly. 'The tropics are beautiful, but the humidity would get me down. Give me an English drizzle any day!'

She waited for him to say he hoped to see her once she was home, but he silently led her across the grass to the far end of the gardens. Nestled in the undergrowth and illuminated by the moon, was a small pond, and floating in its centre was a water lily, its white-and-yellow petals folded for the night on its broad green bed of leaves.

'How perfect,' Sharon murmured, entranced.

'It's the golden water lily,' he explained. 'I wanted you to see it because it reminds me of you.'

It was an unexpected compliment and she didn't know what to say. Silently she listened to the buzz of insects and the strains of violin music wafting across the scented night air. It was a Somerset Maugham setting, she thought, with herself as one of his luckless heroines.

Yet the magic of the night held less magic for her

than the man beside her. He was the enchantment and the spell. She had been aware of it from the first, and tonight it was enhanced by the knowledge that come the morrow he would be thousands of miles away.

Would he kiss her goodbye? she wondered. She wanted him to, yet was afraid, knowing his touch would arouse her to a response she might not easily forget. Yet to forget him was essential, for he would forget *her*. But at this particular moment she was aware only of his closeness, the musky smell of him that made her whole body tingle and ache to be held in his arms.

Luckily he did not guess, and walked round the edge of the pond, and further along the lawns.

'Come and sit over here,' he called, and she followed him to a bench perched on a hillock overlooking the river. She settled down beside him and gazed out at the shining dark water.

'You have the gift of silence,' he murmured after a few moments. 'A rare quality in a woman.'

'I always thought I talked too much,' she confessed.

'Only when you've something to say. But you don't twitter.' He half-turned to study her. 'I'd have thought hotel work too limiting for someone of your temperament. Didn't you ever consider taking up a profession?'

'Running a hotel *is* a profession.'

'Sorry,' he apologised. 'You're right. What I meant was, a profession that would stretch you more.'

'Nothing could stretch me more than hotel management,' she said firmly. 'It's not *one* profession, Kane, it's half-a-dozen! You have to keep accounts, learn to work in the dining room, have an excellent understanding of cookery, know how to be a chambermaid and what it entails to be a receptionist. Then you must learn to control staff, manage your guests and promote your hotel.' Breathless, she stopped. 'And that's just for starters!'

'Then I think I'll stick to Morgan Construction!'

'Wise of you,' she said, and saw him smile.

He made no further comment and sat quietly beside her, his hands buried in the pockets of his jacket, his body reclining against the seat. It was all she could do not to reach out and touch his hair or stroke his cheek, with its faintly discernible shadow. Unexpectedly she remembered how devastated she had been when Pete had left. Yet now it seemed like a dream and, like a dream, unreal. She had never really loved him, she knew that now. She had merely needed someone to love *her*. But it was different with Kane. Even to think of him loving her was so far-fetched as to be impossible! It was a good thing he was leaving. No matter how firm her resolve not to fall in love with him, a few weeks in his company and she would have been lost for all time.

'I really *have* to go in now,' she said, rising.

'You use the clock like some women use headaches!' he drawled. 'If you want to leave, say so.'

'I don't want to leave,' she protested. 'But it's after midnight.'

'See?' he chuckled, and returned with her to the hotel.

She walked quickly, not wanting him to think she was angling for a kiss, and all too soon they were in the lobby which, even at this hour, was milling with people. She stopped by the elevator and held out her hand.

'Goodbye, Kane. Have a safe journey.'

'Not so fast, darling.' He kept her hand in his. 'I'm coming up too.'

Scarlet-cheeked, she went into the elevator. Naturally he wanted to go up; he was leaving the hotel at the crack of dawn. Silently she stared at the lights flashing the floors. Third, fourth . . . Only a few more to go and they would be parting for ever. The doors slid back and she turned stiffly towards him, but he took her arm and went out with her.

'Which is your room?'

'At the end. But there's no need to walk all the way with me.'

He ignored her, and her heart began beating wildly. She took out her key and held it ready, anxious to get the final moment over with. Putting it in the lock, she opened the door and left it slightly ajar before extending her hand for the second time.

Instead of taking it, he pushed her inside and followed her. As she swung round to protest, he pulled her into his arms, the hardness of his body pressing against hers.

'Did you think you could get rid of me so easily?' There was laughter in his voice. 'At least give me a goodbye kiss.'

Tilting her chin, he lowered his head to her mouth. Its gentle touch surprised her, as did the absence of passion. It was a kiss that held only warmth and affection.

'We'll be more comfortable on the settee,' he murmured, lifting her up.

'No,' she protested, kicking out with her feet. 'Put me down.'

He proceeded to do so, but on the settee, and sank down with her. Both his arms came around her, and with a sigh she leaned against his chest, her head finding its rightful place. But only for a second, for he lifted her face to his and started kissing her again. This time it was different. Desire had hardened, as was evidenced by his body, and though she tried not to respond, she was no match for the passion he skilfully aroused in her.

Her lips parted, and his tongue sought refuge in the dark warmth, probing and darting until she was aflame for him. Convulsively she clutched him closer, trembling as he slipped her low-necked dress from her shoulders to disclose the fullness of breasts barely hidden by a wisp of lace.

'God! you're beautiful,' he groaned. 'I never imagined . . .'

Pushing her away from him, he eased her back upon the cushions and feasted his eyes on her. Colour flooded her face at the undisguised sensuality on his, and she shrank back.

'Don't be ashamed because I'm looking at you,' he whispered. 'A body like yours was made to be looked at.'

'I'm not a statue,' she said huskily.

'That I know. You're warm and real. Made for holding, touching.'

His hands lightly stroked the swelling curves, and she put up her hands to stop him. But he stayed the movement, then stifled her protest with his mouth, his tongue once more arousing her to mindless ecstasy as his hands continued their caressing; stroking their skin, gently feathering her nipples into peaks of desire that made her gasp and tremble, cry out for him to hold her tighter and assuage the desire that coursed through her like a flame.

Yet even as she heard her low moans of passion, sanity returned and, with it, self-reproach that she had let herself be carried away by his desire for her. Were he in love with her, she would have had no regrets, but knowing it was simply lust . . .

With all her strength she pushed him back, at the same time trying to twist her body away from his. For a moment she thought he was going to resist, then he pushed himself away from her. His face was flushed and damp, his shirt undone—by her or him, she wasn't sure—and the buckle of his belt open.

'No?' he questioned thickly.

'No, Kane. I'm sorry.'

'Me too. I thought you wanted me.'

Wanted. Not loved. Thank heavens he didn't know how closely she had come to loving him. But love needed time to develop, to deepen from desire into a more lasting emotion, and time was something Kane could not spare. Even when he did, she doubted if he would want a relationship that demanded the kind of commitment she was looking for. Work would always take precedence with him, and a wife would be of secondary importance.

'Let me love you properly,' he murmured. 'I want you so much.'

'I can't,' she said huskily, half-turning away from him. 'I'm sorry if I gave you the wrong impression.'

'So am I. Just now you were so responsive, so demanding.' He caught her chin and tilted her face towards him. 'Why did you change you mind about going through with it?'

'Maybe because I never have,' she confessed.

'*What?*' He sat up straight. 'You mean . . . But you can't be! Not in this day and age.'

'In *this* day and age,' she stated. 'I haven't, and I still am.'

'I see.' He rose, one long-fingered hand raking back his ruffled hair. The bronze skin of his chest glistened faintly with perspiration, and he grimaced as he buttoned his shirt.

'I'm not lying,' she said. 'I'd like you to believe me.'

'I do. No girl would make up such a thing! I know I called you an innocent, but I didn't realise you were still a virgin. It's not so laudable, you know. Life is meant to be lived, Sharon, not watched from the sidelines.'

'I agree. But there's a right and a wrong time to be a player!'

'I take it you don't want to play with *me*?'

'I don't want to play with anyone who's still playing the field.'

His mouth curved with faint amusement. 'You're missing a lot of fun.'

'It wouldn't be, for me. Sex without love is meaningless, Kane.'

'Okay, you've made your point.' Lithely he went to the door. 'I know when I'm not wanted, sweetheart. And I'm sorry you feel like this. You'd have enjoyed it and so would I.'

'Try vanilla ice-cream next time,' she said.

His eyes darkened. 'That wasn't a nice thing to say, Sharon. But I'll forgive you.' Picking up his jacket, he went out, closing the door quietly behind him.

Sharon felt sick. She wanted to run after him and call him back, but common sense told her it was better to let it end this way. After all, she barely knew him. What she felt was sexual attraction—nothing more.

Even as she tried to convince herself of this, she knew she was being far from truthful, and that her heart rejected what her mind was urging her to do. No matter what logic said, Kane Morgan already meant too much to her, and it was going to take all her determination to forget him.

CHAPTER EIGHT

SHARON had little time to dwell on Kane's departure, for even as his private jet took off from the airport, Mr Bim called her into his office and told her she was being sent to the Avonmore at Pattaya the following day.

She was delighted by the prospect of leaving the city, convinced new surroundings would help her forget Kane. Pattaya was some eighty miles from Bangkok on the Gulf of Thailand, and was the country's most popular beach resort, with luxury hotels and villas, white sands, and coral islands lying just off the coast.

'How long will I be staying there?' she asked.

'Until the rainy season starts.'

She was turning to leave when he called her back. 'By the way, one of our interpreters is off sick, and I'd like you to stand in for her today. She was taking a party of French people round the city with a guide. But his English is poor, and his French non-existent, so he'll need someone to interpret for him.'

'*My* French is far from perfect,' Sharon said, delighted to have another chance of seeing around Bangkok, 'but I'll do my best. What time are we due to leave?'

'Five minutes ago!'

With a laugh, she spun round and hurried out.

It was indeed an ideal way to spend her last day here, and as the air-conditioned coach rumbled down the drive an hour later, Sharon gave heartfelt thanks to the interpreter's indisposition.

Their first stop was Wat Arun, the five-towered

Temple of Dawn on the south side of the river. Its central tower thrust 260 feet into the sky, and the walls and roofs glittered with tiny shards of pottery and porcelain, as if a thousand dinner plates had been smashed and placed there.

Inside, it resembled any other Buddhist shrine, with its proliferation of gold ornaments and large, golden Buddha sitting high in the place of honour. The temple was a hive of activity, with dozens of tourists milling about, though the densest crowds were to be found at the souvenir stalls in front of the entrance, where wide-brimmed reed hats, embroidered bags and gilt jewellery were available in profusion.

Several of the tourists remarked cynically on the lack of reverence, and Sharon felt like reminding them that Lourdes, in France, was equally as commercial.

The next part of their journey was through the district of Thom Buri, where she knew they would be going again tomorrow when they visited the Floating Market.

'You'll have to leave the hotel very early in the morning, though,' she warned, 'because the market's almost over by nine!' She indicated the broad, grey-green ribbon of water. 'There'll hardly be a metre of space out there tomorrow, it will be so full of sampans—those are flat-bottomed canoes—selling vegetables.'

'What they don't sell, they can tip in the river,' one of the women commented.

Everyone laughed, and a youngish looking Frenchman took the opportunity to leave his seat and take an empty one nearer to Sharon. He was of average height and in his early thirties, with limpid brown eyes that reminded her of Sacha Distel.

'I noticed you in the bar last night with Mr Morgan,' he murmured to her as they alighted from the coach a little later, and followed the guide along a narrow street lined with shops, their windows eye-catching with paper dragons, bottles of snake wine and strings of noodles.

'How well do you know him?' he went on.

Alerted by his interest in Kane, and recollecting all she had read about industrial espionage, Sharon grew cautious.

'I met him at the hotel,' she said. 'How well do *you* know him?'

'By sight and repute only. I'm here to protect the interests of a French consortium,' the man confided. 'Which reminds me, Tassy Bonlam is giving a party for all the contractors tonight. Perhaps you'd care to come along as my guest?'

Sharon was tempted, for she was curious to meet the Thai girl. Yet even as she went to say 'Yes', caution won the day.

'I'm afraid I can't, Monsieur——?'

'Calvez. Leon Calvez.' He gave a slight bow. 'If you should change your mind . . .'

'I doubt I will. I'm leaving for Pattaya tomorrow morning, and I've my packing to do.'

Before he could press her further, the guide halted outside a Chinese restaurant, and Sharon announced they were stopping here for lunch and would have an hour free afterwards for shopping.

Still intent on pursuing her, Leon Calvez made sure he sat beside her, and paid flattering attention to her throughout the meal. She tried to ignore him, and the more persistent he became, the more she remembered Kane's lingering kisses and sensuous touch. Had she been childish not to let him love her completely? Yet if she had, how would she be feeling today? Completely female—that went without saying—but also tarnished, used. She sighed, accepting she would always feel like

this if she gave herself to a man who merely regarded her as a body to possess.

'I beg your pardon?' With a start she realised the Frenchman was speaking to her again.

'I was saying Mr Morgan must have given up hope of getting the contract. I hear he's returned to London.'

'Because he had urgent business there,' she said abruptly.

'I see.' His eyes narrowed. 'But I imagine Miss Bonlam was surprised. I believe she and Mr Morgan were—how you say it?—"very good friends".'

Sharon remained silent.

'Which shows how astute he is,' the man went on. 'They say she has considerable influence over her father.'

'Then why don't *you* try chatting her up?' Sharon asked bluntly, and turning her back on him, concentrated on the woman on her other side.

Lunch over, Leon Calvez took the hint and left her alone, and Sharon escorted several of the tourists to buy lengths of Thai silk, and then to a fruit stall where they bought plastic bags filled with pineapple chunks—and ice cubes to keep them cool—which they ate as they wandered back through the crowds to the coach.

Early next morning she boarded an air-conditioned bus for Pattaya, in the company of twenty guests who were spending the last half of their holiday by the sea.

The three-hour journey was mostly through flat countryside and paddy fields, and there was little to see. Here and there one glimpsed men and women wading in streams as they cast fine-meshed nets to catch tiny fish, and the occasional village they passed through offered it to them crisply fried and served on palm leaves!

The bus driver—anxious to earn a tip—pointed out the tiny 'spirit houses' outside many of the homes. Sharon was reminded of the bird baths often found in British gardens, though these were slightly larger and shaped like miniature temples. They were supposed to provide a resting place for the guardian spirit that watched over the family living in the house, and each day flowers and candles were placed beside it, as well as rice and fruit for the spirit's nourishment.

It was nearly noon when they bowled into the village of Pattaya. It was larger than Sharon had expected—a town almost—though she rightly guessed that a few years ago, before the advent of the luxury hotels bordering the shoreline, it had been the same as the other sleepy hamlets through which they had passed.

A long, winding main street, filled with large stores, was punctuated by smaller streets where the shops were the one-roomed structures she had come to expect. Dressmakers abounded, and Sharon determined that on her first free day she would come here and replenish her wardrobe. After all, it was crazy not to take advantage of the fabulous materials and handmade clothes—they'd cost ten times more in Britain!

A few minutes out of the village and they were driving along the sea front. To the right lay the wide sweep of the Gulf of Thailand, a grey-blue expanse of water lapping a brilliant white sandy beach, while on the left ranged rows of luxury villas. Gradually these gave way to the hotels, one glittering edifice after another breaking the lapis lazuli sky. Although Sharon knew she was being a traitor to her profession, she could not help wishing she had seen Pattaya before the travel trade had discovered it!

The Avonmore was set in four acres of landscaped grounds, interspersed with a vast kidney-shaped swimming pool, and a smaller one for children, as well as an open-air bar around which tables with large, colourful umbrellas were set.

Inside, the hotel bore the same stamp as its sister one in Bangkok, though the fabrics on the cushions and settees were gaily flowered, and there was a greater expanse of terrazzo and marble flooring.

Sharon's room was larger than the one in Bangkok, but had no balcony, and being at the side of the building she had to crane her neck out of the window to glimpse the sea. A notice on the wall advised the window be kept shut to keep out insects, and obeying the injunction she set the air-conditioning on 'high' and started unpacking. She never felt at home until her personal things were around her, and she placed a photograph of her parents on the dressing table and gazed at it for a long while, suddenly overcome by homesickness.

She heard from them regularly, mostly news about the farm and village, and consumed every word, amazed how even the most banal news took on a special flavour when one was miles away in a foreign land. Jet travel had widened one's horizons, but on the negative side it had widened the gap between families, encouraging young ones to move away, and leave elderly parents and relatives alone. She sighed, knowing her introspection was caused in part by a tall, black-haired man with a cool gaze and even cooler heart. A man of passion, but not of love.

'Get out of my mind, Kane Morgan!' she said aloud. 'I barely know you and I've no intention of letting you haunt me!'

On which determined note she donned a jaunty red cotton dress and went down to introduce herself to the manager.

She was delighted when he turned out to be a friendly American not more than ten years older than herself. Who was it said the Avonmore never promoted young people?

'I haven't been here long,' Bud Cameron explained, guessing her thoughts. 'The guy I replaced was too regimental for the Thais. They're a hot-tempered lot under their phlegmatic exterior, so don't be fooled by their gentle manner.'

'I don't think it's hot temper so much as pride,' Sharon demurred, recalling what Mr Chittiwera had told her about his countryman's character. 'Never make them feel small nor step out of your class,' she quoted.

'Easier said than done,' Bud Cameron drawled. 'The distinctions in a hotel can be more marked than the Civil Service!'

'I know.' Sharon's blue eyes sparkled. 'The head waiter won't eat with the commis boys, and the chefs won't eat with anyone!'

'Well, to be honest, those sort of demarcations don't bother me. My main problem is shortage of decent domestic staff. They all prefer working in Bangkok, so I'm forced to recruit them from the surrounding villages.'

'Is that difficult?'

'No. There are plenty available. But they're totally untrained.'

'But once they are, you——'

'Once they are, they move to the capital, and we begin all over again!'

'I see.'

'I'm glad you do,' he said dryly, 'because the two of us may frequently have to fill in!'

Sharon grinned. 'I'm ready to put my hand to anything.'

'I'll hold you to that. Meantime, I want you to act as hostess and enjoy yourself with the guests. Many of them come here on non-package trips and don't know how to fill in their time.'

'Don't know?' Her eyes wandered to the sparkling pool, and beyond it to the beach, glimpsed through the palm trees.

'Not everyone likes sunbathing,' Bud Cameron chided, reading her thoughts. 'Some guests only seem to come for the shopping!'

'I quite like that myself!'

'Then you'll have a great time here. But any problems, don't hesitate to tell me.'

Sharon could not envisage any, for the atmosphere in the hotel was extremely relaxed. Guests wandered around in shorts and swimsuits, dressing up only for dinner, which was invariably taken around the poolside, the surrounding trees lit by coloured lanterns. Truly paradise on earth—if you could afford the price!

On her third day she took several women into the village, travelling in local taxis: small, open-sided vans with seats in the back, protected from the heat by little draped curtains, which blew around wildly as the drivers careered along at a hair-raising speed.

On second viewing, the old and new sections of Pattaya were quite distinct, and most tourists preferred the older, despite its dusty, potholed road, narrow pavements and shallow gutter. At least there was life here, and the shops were full of the usual gilt and silver bowls and plates, cotton table mats and cloths, and wood carvings.

At the northern end of the street sprawled the market, half of it enclosed, half open to the sky. Here there were fantastic displays of vegetables, fruits, nuts and spices, their colours echoed in the bright cheongsams worn by the women. It was a wonderful scene for a painting, Sharon thought, and vowed to look for one to take home to her parents.

Though her work kept her busy, she still missed Kane, and was furious that despite their short acquaintance he had made such an impact on her. Was it because she knew he was powerful, unattached and hard to get? Would she feel the same if he were a bank clerk or a salesman? Even as she posed the question she knew the answer. The character of the man made him what he was, and his character was part of his charisma. Wherever Kane was and whatever he did, he would be successful, that was certain. Equally certain was that he had gone from her life.

The only thing she regretted was not accepting Leon Calvez's invitation to Tassy Bonlam's party. It would have been interesting to meet the girl who had been Kane's 'good friend'. Still, the Bonlams had a villa in Pattaya, and Tassy was bound to come into the hotel sooner or later.

During her second week at the resort, half the guests left and a new contingent arrived. While they settled in, Sharon was kept busy rearranging rooms, finding lost luggage, booking tours for the following day for people who were only staying for three or four, and seeing that those who wanted to dine al fresco were allocated tables outside.

It was well into the afternoon before she managed to get a breather, and donning a swimsuit she went into the garden. Several of the guests asked her to join them, but she refused. Quite a few men were here on their own—American and English bachelors working in Thailand—and she could not help being flattered by their attention. She knew—without conceit—that her colouring and height set her apart from most women, and dressed to show it off to best advantage.

Today she wore a peacock blue one piece that modestly covered her body yet outlined every beautiful curve. Its colour matched her eyes and the sapphire stones at her ears, which she had bought in the hotel boutique. They had been staggeringly expensive, but as she had received a substantial rise in salary, she had decided to spoil herself. Well, why not? she had thought at the time. She did not have a man to do it for her!

Lying on a chaise longue, she listened to the splashing and laughter around her. In next to no time she was asleep, only awakening when someone called her name and she opened her eyes to see the manager looking down at her.

'Don't bother moving,' he said as she hurriedly went to rise. 'I'm on my way to take a look at our shopping parade——' his hand indicated a row of newly built boutiques beyond the trees—'and seeing you here reminded me to tell you I'll be needing more help from you during the next few days.'

'Staff problems?' she grimaced.

'More likely guest problems. A large contingent's arriving after the weekend. Men only,' he added. 'They'll be here a few weeks, so I'd like you to lay on some entertainment.'

'Are they on holiday or business?'

'Business. They're competing for the highway contract, and final tenders have to be in before the end of the month. You probably saw some of the groups when you were in Bangkok. Mr Bonlam's spending his vacation here, so they've all followed him down.'

'They'll probably be following him back to Bangkok too,' she said dryly. 'The Minister enjoys making them sweat it out!'

Bud Cameron looked quizzical. 'Is that inside information?'

'It's bitter knowledge among the delegates,' she replied.

'Well, it's good for *our* business, so why worry!' The manager moved off, then paused. 'If you're at a loose end one evening, come over for a coffee and meet my wife. Any of the bell boys will take you to our bungalow. It's only a few minutes' walk from here.'

Thanking him, Sharon promised she would. Bud Cameron was the youngest and friendliest manager she had worked with, though his genial manner was a front for a highly demanding boss. One thing she had learned from him though: give your orders with a smile, and if you *should* lose your temper, do it quietly!

On Sunday, Sharon organised the staff to prepare for the new arrivals, fleetingly wondering whether Mark Victorsen and his family would be among them. She hoped not, for it would remind her of Kane. As if she needed reminding!

Remembering the delegates were all rivals, she gave the Japanese contingent the floor with the most available free rooms, since they generally travelled in large parties; and the Italians—who were a noisy bunch—she placed in the new wing nearest the boutiques, which were open until late at night. At least they'd get a taste of their own medicine!

First thing Monday, she inspected the rooms to ensure everything was in order. Fruit and flowers stood on each bedside table and the refrigerators were stocked with spirits, beer and soft drinks.

The Swedish delegation arrived first, followed almost at once by the Canadians. The Japanese were expected at mid-afternoon and Sharon was right in assuming they would be a large party, for a call from

Bangkok confirmed there were fifteen in all. They were prepared to share double rooms, except for the leader of the group who wished to have his own.

She was at Reception when they arrived. Fourteen men in navy suits and thick-lensed spectacles, all hovering anxiously near the entrance, unwilling to check in before their superior did so.

As she moved forward to greet them, porters laden with luggage pushed through the doors, followed by a tall, athletic figure with silver-fair hair and freckles. Pete Wilburg! She stopped dead in her tracks. What one earth was *he* doing here?

It was hard to say who was the more surprised, though Pete regained his composure first, and strode forward with a broad smile.

'Sharon! By all that's wonderful Are you here on vacation?'

'Not exactly,' she said, managing a smile. 'This is my job. But what about you?'

'I'm working too. I'm heading the Japanese delegation.'

She was astonished. 'I thought you were with an American company?'

'I got a better offer.' He was still beaming at her as he went over to his party and spoke to them, after which they all surged forward to register.

'I hope we'll see something of each other while I'm here?' he went on, returning to her side.

'I'm assigned to look after *all* the delegates,' she said coolly, 'so it's quite likely.'

'That wasn't what I had in mind,' he murmured. 'Or are your affections already taken?'

'I'm a career girl,' she responded.

'I know. That was the trouble.'

'Come off it, Pete. Even if I hadn't been, we'd only have been friends.'

'Or lovers,' he said softly. 'But you turned me down. Still would, I suppose?'

Silently she headed for the elevator. 'If you and your group would like to follow me, I'll show you your rooms.'

Going up to their floor, Pete stood close beside her, eyeing her so intently she was relieved when they could get out. Pete's room was last along the corridor and overlooked the sea. White-capped waves broke on the shoreline, and above it a host of red-and-white parachutes floated in the clear blue sky.

'What are those?' he asked.

'Parasails. You're harnessed into a parachute and a motor-boat takes you round the bay. The faster it goes the higher you rise.'

'Seems like fun. I must try it. I suppose you're having a marvellous time here?'

'It makes a change from London. But it's hard work.' She paused. 'I've been promised managership when I get back.'

'Great!' Pete came close to her. 'But I still think you're wasted working. You should be making a man happy.'

'I'm making *hundreds* of men happy!' she retorted.

Grinning, he went across to the small refrigerator. 'How about a drink to celebrate our unexpected reunion?'

'Not now, thanks. I'm on duty.'

'Still as proper as ever I see! Then how about going out with me later?'

'I'm not sure when I'm free,' she prevaricated. 'I don't have set hours when the hotel's full.'

'You giving me the brush off?'

'Of course not.'

She wondered what she had ever seen in him. He was good looking, of course, yet he left her cold. Not so him, it appeared, for he reached out for her and kissed her full on the mouth. She tried to respond but it was hopeless when the very touch of him reminded her of the last man who had held her. Kane Morgan, who dwarfed Pete in everything but size.

'What's wrong, Sharon?' Pete asked as he drew back. 'Kissing not allowed either, when on duty?'

'How clever of you to guess!' She went to the door, but he was ahead of her, barring her way.

'I *do* want to see you, Sharon. Can't we fix a definite time?'

'I told you I can't right now. But you'll be seeing me around, so we can arrange it later.'

'I hope you mean that.' Lightly he touched her cheek, letting his fingers trail down the side of her neck. 'I've missed you, angel. Much more than I thought I would. Have you missed *me*?'

'I did in the beginning,' she confessed. 'But not since coming here.'

'I hate it when you're truthful!'

She laughed, and after a brief pause, so did he, though she sensed he was not genuinely amused. It obviously hurt his ego to think she could forget him so easily. Recollecting the months of anguish she had suffered because of him—indeed until she had met Kane in fact—she vowed never to let Pete mean anything to her again. Not that he could when her whole being clamoured for a man who had merely seen her as a one-night stand!

'Tell me,' Pete said, opening the door for her, 'Do I have many other competitors here?'

'For me, or for the contract?' she flashed sarcastically.

He had the grace to redden. 'For the contract, actually.'

'The hotel's swarming with them,' she replied.

'I see. Would you know if Morgan Construction is

here? I heard they were in with a good chance.'

'We've no booking for them in Pattaya.'

'I'm sure they'll be here. Morgan won't miss a battle like this.'

'He had to go back to London,' she said without thinking, and saw the surprise on Pete's face.

'You *know* him?'

'He was at the Avonmore in Bangkok when I was there.'

'I see. Any idea why he left?'

'No,' she lied, and changed the subject. 'How long do you think you'll be staying here, Pete?'

'Depends on Bonlam. He enjoys making you sweat it out.'

'Kane thought so too,' Sharon commented, and could have bitten out her tongue as Pete raised his eyebrows at her.

'On first name terms, were you?'

'That's not unusual these days,' she parried.

'And especially with Morgan,' came the reply. 'Compared with him, I'm a monk!' He bent his head to kiss her again, but she evaded him and opened the door.

'There's a gala dinner tonight, with some beautiful Thai dancers. Shall I book a table for you and your group?'

'I won't be eating with them,' he said. 'I prefer to keep my distance. Anyway, I want to take you out alone tonight. I've had my fill of Thai dancing.'

'How come?'

'I was here two years ago on a project. Nothing came of it, but I got to learn some intricate dance steps!'

'I'm sure they can teach you plenty more!'

'I'd rather learn from you,' he said, reaching for her again.

Evading him, she made for the elevator, aware that her coolness was having the opposite effect from what she intended. Poor Pete. He would have to learn the hard way that he could not pick up their relationship where he had left off.

Returning to the lobby, she revelled in the knowledge that he meant nothing to her, and wondered how long it would be before she could say the same about Kane Morgan.

CHAPTER NINE

THE moment Kane boarded the plane taking him to Bangkok, he felt suppressed excitement build up in him that had nothing to do with the prospect of winning the highway contract. Of course he knew what it was: the knowledge that within hours he would be seeing Sharon. He had a clear image of her, and was acutely aware that she had dominated his subconscious even while he had been trying to forget her. It seemed he wasn't as adept at controlling his emotions as he thought!

He knew there was only way to rid himself of his obsession for her: get her into bed! Strange he had not made a more concerted effort that night in Bangkok. It wasn't like him to be easily foiled. But her apparent innocence had inhibited him, and even now he was uncertain whether she had been truthful or had made a fool of him. Girls were adept at putting on an act, and it was hard to credit that someone as lovely and liberated as she appeared, was as untouched as she professed.

Well, there was one way to find out. He would put her to the test! The thought stirred his senses; his desire to possess her had intensified with time, not lessened, and this unusual phenomenon he found intensely annoying.

He tried to pretend it was because she had played hard to get, but he was too honest to believe it. Strangely, much as he wanted her physically, he wanted her company too. Sharon was never boring. She could talk on a host of subjects and her comments about his work had been perceptive. Tassy Bonlam was no slouch in the intelligence stakes either, yet there was something about the Thai girl—for all her gentle manner and soft-spokenness—that made him wary.

As the plane took off, he mused upon the change in himself and how introspective he had become. He had always had a natural curiosity about people and events and, in the past, would have been chatting up the stewardess; made a date with her probably. She was a lovely brunette and he had always been partial to them. Yet now all he wanted was to bury his face in hair the colour of ripe corn. And you couldn't, he thought wryly, get cornier than that!

Accepting a glass of champagne, he tried to concentrate on the *Financial Times*. But his mind kept wandering and eventually he turned and gazed unseeingly out of the window. He knew Mark Victorsen was surprised he was returning so soon, for his assistant had assured him there was no need to hurry back.

'Bonlam's still meeting other companies,' he had said over the telephone, 'and you might as well wait until a decision's imminent, before returning.'

But Kane had been too restless to remain in London and once the Welsh contract had been finalised, he had booked his flight. Normally he supervised a new operation for the first month or two, but he could not envisage any problems arising with this one. Anyway, if they did, he would return. But as of now, Sharon was his main concern, and the need to hold her, to make her respond to him, was uppermost in his mind.

Another forty-eight hours and he would know if he had built up his hopes too high. After all, she might be a total disaster sexually! He almost hoped she was, for it would be the best way of getting her out of his system. Sighing, he drained his drink, refused another, and lowered his chair into the sleep position, requesting the stewardess not to wake him up for any meals. If things went according to his hopes, he would need all the sleep he could get!

He was feeling refreshed and on top of the world when Mark met him at the airport next morning and filled him in on events of the past two days.

'Barchard Construction are here from Huston, and Pete Wilburg's heading a Japanese outfit. *He's* going to be our toughest competition. They all moved out to Pattaya yesterday,' the man added. 'That's where Bonlam's carrying on his negotiations, so we'll have to go there too.'

Kane was dismayed. Yet he could not admit it to Mark without disclosing feelings he had no desire to uncover. The contract had to come first. When he had won—or lost it—he would have time to pursue the girl who had brought him back here.

'You'd better fix our reservations then,' he said.

'I've already done so.'

'Good.' Kane hesitated, then lost the battle with himself. 'I'll join you there tomorrow. You can hold the fort till then.' He paused. 'Your son should enjoy it better there. Most kids like the beach.'

'He and Angela have gone home. Terry had to start school.'

'Oh, right. Guess I'm not *au fait* with term times!'

The Avonmore came in sight and Kane's heart started pounding. He wondered what Sharon's reaction would be when she saw him. Pleasure or indifference? After all, he had been away more than five weeks. Still, one thing was sure; she would never pretend. She was too honest for that.

He leapt from the car as it stopped and hurried into the lobby, leaving Mark to handle the luggage. Going straight to Reception, he asked for her.

'Miss Kingston is no longer with us,' the clerk said.

'What?' Kane was thunderstruck. Don't say he had flown half-way across the world to find she was back in England! Or had the man who had made her wary of relationships—she had practically admitted she had been let down in love—suddenly realised what he was missing and come after her?

'When did she leave the company?' he asked.

'She hasn't left us, sir,' the clerk smiled. 'She's been transferred to our hotel in Pattaya.'

Relief—swift as a flash flood—encompassed Kane. It looked as though Fate was rooting for him after all! Striding across to Mark, he told him he had changed his mind and would go to Pattaya at once.

Used to his boss' lightning changes of mind, the older man signalled for the luggage to be returned to the car, and within minutes they were speeding towards the coast.

For the first part of the journey Kane listened to details about the negotiations, but half-way through he feigned fatigue and closed his eyes, wanting time to ponder his reaction when he had thought Sharon was no longer free.

In seconds he had ricocheted from disappointment to elation and then despair. Disappointment that he would not be seeing her, elation that he was saved from making a fool of himself over a girl, and despair at knowing he *wanted* to be a fool! God! what had she done to him? She had found a chink in his armour, penetrated his defences and wrapped herself around his heart. His desire for her had developed into 'I can't live without her', though he had not realised it until he had heard the clerk say she had gone. Mulling it over as the car ate up the miles to the coast, he wryly admitted that the biter had finally been bit. He was in love!

They reached Pattaya at three. Kane had first come
here as a guest of the Minister, which was when he
had met Tassy, and he had spent several soul-
searching hours debating whether to ask her to marry
him. But even at the height of her attraction for him,
something had told him it would not work. Now he
knew why. Though he had wanted her physically, she
had aroused no tenderness in him. Funny, when she
was so tiny and fragile. Yet Sharon, tall, stately
Sharon of the voluptuous body and shy eyes, filled
him with a desire to protect.

The Avonmore gleamed white ahead of him, and as
the car drew to a stop, Kane jumped out and made
straight for Reception. Abruptly he asked where Miss
Kingston was, uncaring what anyone thought of his
impatience to see her.

'She's at the pool,' the clerk said in answer to his
question. 'Shall I page her for you?'

'No. On second thoughts I think I'll go to my room
first and shower. I've had a long flight.'

He was delighted Mark had managed to fix him up
with a penthouse suite here too, and within a short
space of time he had unpacked and was stepping into
the glass-cubicled shower. He was glad he had not
gone rushing after Sharon. He needed time to
compose himself, not go rushing after her like a
lovesick schoolboy. But even as he told himself this, he
found his hands shaking, and he was in and out of the
shower in sixty seconds flat. So much for his
determination not to rush!

Female heads turned as he walked across the terrace
and down the steps to the pool. It was huge and free
form, and there seemed to be hundreds of lounging
chairs and gaily coloured mattresses ranged around it,
most of them occupied. But he could not see Sharon
anywhere.

Slowly he circled the perimeter, wending his way between tables and striped umbrellas, where guests sat drinking and nibbling titbits. Then suddenly his eye was caught by some striped mattresses half-hidden by a clump of flowering bushes, and he heard soft, warm laughter. Careful not to intrude, he moved away. The laughter came again, and something about it made him step closer and part the leaves.

Sharon, in a miniscule green sundress, was lounging on one of the mattresses, her back towards him, her corn gold hair catching the sun. A man lay beside her on another mattress, and as Kane watched, he pulled her sharply to him and kissed her full on the mouth.

Kane was not aware of making a sound. Yet he must have done, for she quickly turned her head in his direction. The sun was in her eyes and for an instant she did not see who it was, then recognition dawned, followed by a look of amazement.

Murmuring something to the man, she jumped up and came towards him. 'Hello, Kane. I didn't know you were coming back.'

He forced himself to return her smile. 'I settled my affairs quicker than I thought.' He glanced at the other man, hiding the swift fury he felt as he recognised him. 'Hello, Wilburg. So we're competitors again!'

'For the contract or for Sharon?' Pete drawled.

'I'm not up for bids,' Sharon interposed sweetly. 'I consider myself priceless!'

'All lovely women are,' Kane said smoothly, delighted to find he was in control of himself. 'Maybe we'll have a drink later. You're busy now, I see.'

Not giving her a chance to reply, he walked on. Disappointment and anger stiffened his throat and he swallowed hard. He had only himself to blame, going in search of her like a love-crazed adolescent. He should have played it cool, pretended to be surprised when he met her inside. At least then he'd have been spared the sight of her flirting with another man. He swore under his breath. She was no better than any other woman!

Mark was waiting for him in his suite, relaxing in a cane chair on the patio overlooking the sea, and sipping a Scotch and soda.

'Seen any of the other delegates yet?'

'Only Pete Wilburg. He was with Sharon Kingston, the girl from the Avonmore in Bangkok.'

'I forgot to mention she was here.' The older man's expression was cautious.

'Why should you?' Kane said off-handedly. 'Hotel staff are always shunted around.'

'Trust Wilburg to cotton on to the prettiest girl here,' Mark added. 'He's a smooth operator. Almost *your* match!'

Kane shrugged. 'I can't see any of us having much time for women down here. Does Bonlam know I'm back?'

'Sure. I told——' Mark broke off as the phone rang. He picked it up and spoke into it, then held it out. 'For you,' he said.

Kane knew instantly who it was, and kept his tone casual as he spoke Sharon's name.

'I th-thought that—that if you were free,' she stammered, 'I—er—I'd come up to see you.'

'I'd like that very much, but not now I'm afraid. I'm in conference.'

'Later then?'

'I may be tied up all day. But I'll be in touch.'

How easy it was to feign indifference! He was almost convincing himself; and Sharon too from the tone of her voice as she said goodbye. Yet she had only herself to blame. If she chose to flirt with Wilburg, he'd leave her to it.

'You were rather off-hand,' Mark remarked. 'I thought you fancied her.'

'No more than any other pretty girl. Which reminds me, is Tassy in Pattaya?'

'Yes. Do you want me to call her for you?'

'I'll do it myself. I'll meet you up here in an hour. I need a chance to relax.'

The man departed and a few seconds later Kane was speaking to Tassy. Yes, she would be free to dine with him that evening, and was delighted he was back.

'And that puts "finis" to you, Sharon Kingston,' Kane said as he replaced the receiver. 'It's not only a woman who can wash someone out of her hair!'

CHAPTER TEN

SHARON put down the receiver, overwhelmingly depressed. It had been foolish of her to ring Kane, but she had not anticipated such a curt response from him, even though he *had* found her with another man. At least he should have given her the chance to explain Pete was an old friend and did not mean anything to her now.

Dejectedly she wandered back to the pool and rejoined him.

'Everything okay?' he asked.

'Fine,' she lied, sinking on to her mattress. 'I had to finalise the arrangements for tonight's dinner-dance.'

He rolled on to his back and put his hands beneath his head. 'I thought you said you hardly knew Kane Morgan?'

'You thought right.'

'I didn't get that impression from the look on his face.'

'Maybe he didn't expect to find a hotel employee in the arms of a guest!'

Pete chuckled. 'One day someone's going to deflower you!'

'May I ask the relevance of that comment?'

'Simply that I've a feeling Kane Morgan would like it to be *him*.'

'You've a king-sized imagination,' she replied, and rose to move away.

Lithely he followed her and she glanced at him. His skin was more bronzed than when they had met skiing, and his fair hair longer. It gave him a rakish look that was infinitely attractive, yet he still left her cold.

'You used to accuse *me* of having no imagination,' he commented, keeping pace with her.

'I still do, when it comes to people!'

'Always smart with the answer, aren't you?' he grimaced. 'That's what I like about you. You keep me on my toes.'

'I thought it was the opposite. That you'd run a mile from a female who forced you to think!'

'Did I say that? Stupid the things one says in the heat of the moment.'

'Or the reasons one gives for making a quick get-away!'

He had no answer to that and stared straight ahead till they reached the outdoor bar leading into the hotel.

'This is where I leave you, Pete,' she said.

'Join me for a drink first.'

'I've still some things to check over.'

'You mean you aren't dashing up to see Morgan?'

'You do go on about him, don't you?'

'Because I think he's my rival. In business, and with you.' His hand was warm on her arm. 'How about dinner tonight?'

She hesitated. She did not particularly want to see Pete again, yet Kane had been so off-hand, she decided to accept the offer. 'I should be free by seven. I'll meet you here.'

That evening she took special care with her appearance, eventually choosing a dress made for her by a seamstress in the village. Simple in cut—a slim tube that merely hinted at the figure it concealed—it relied for effect on the fabric, the apricot silk giving golden lustre to her hair, which in turn emphasised the blue of her eyes.

She knew she was dressing for Kane, though the

admiration on Pete's face when he saw her was balm to her wounded pride. He could not take his eyes off her, and as she smiled up at him she wished Kane was here to see her. A quick glance round the outdoor bar told her he wasn't, and it was an effort for her to keep the smile on her face. Not that Pete was aware of it; he saw only a beautiful girl whom he was lucky enough to have as his dinner companion.

'What's happened to you?' he asked as he toasted her with his Pimms. 'You look positively glowing. You in love or something?'

'Well, I love being in Pattaya,' she teased. 'But maybe it's the tan I've acquired. A little sunshine can work wonders.'

'Let's see what starlight can do,' he laughed, and leaned forward to squeeze her arm.

Sharon knew it would take more than starlight and Pete to revive her spirits. Indeed a foggy day with a plain man—if one loved him—could be heaven. Quickly she drained her drink, hoping the alcohol would lessen the sharp edge of the pain Kane had inflicted. It was hurt pride, nothing more, and it served her right for thinking anything meaningful could exist between them. She had told herself this the day he had returned to England, but seeing him by the pool so unexpectedly this afternoon had foolishly made her believe he had come back because he had missed her as much as she missed him. Which only went to show what an idiot she was.

'Dinner, I think.' Pete broke into her thoughts. 'I don't know about you, but I'm famished.'

'So am I,' she lied, wondering how she would force down the food.

They left the bar and moved to their table by the poolside. It was a scene of fairy-tale splendour. Soft lights illuminated the trees and cast a gentle glow over the tables, where candle lamps added their own shimmer. Flowers were strewn between the plates, scenting the air, which was already filled with the soft strains of violins played by a group of musicians hidden by the trees.

As Pete set his drink on the table, he moved Sharon's bag to one side. 'What on earth do you have in it?' he laughed, weighing it in his hand. 'The Crown Jewels?'

'Something nearly as valuable,' she said. 'The hotel keys.'

'Good Lord! For *all* the rooms?'

'Except the strong room and kitchens. It's only four master keys, not four hundred!' she explained, seeing his astonishment. 'But Bud Cameron's away for two days, and I'm in charge.'

'Where's his assistant?'

'Gone with him.'

Peter looked impressed. 'So you're top dog now? You're certainly climbing the Avonmore ladder.'

'That's my ambition,' she admitted, knowing it was only partly true. She also wanted a husband and family, and that put Kane right out of the running, for he was the type who would either want his wife to follow him around like a lap dog, or else be content to stay in the background, bringing up the children.

The waiter set the menus before them, and as she picked hers up, she saw Kane a few tables away. In a beige suit, with paler silk shirt, he was far and away the most handsome man here. He also looked the most irritable, if the perfunctory nod he gave his waiter was anything to go by. Did he regret his behaviour to her earlier this afternoon? Hoping so, she gave Pete a brilliant smile. Let Kane put that in his pipe and smoke it!

'May the best company win,' she said, toasting him.

'Then it'll be us,' Pete retorted. 'We're honest, efficient, and as competitive as Morgan Construction. Incidentally, he's sitting not five yards from us, and Tassy Bonlam's just joined him.'

Sharon carefully set her glass on the table, glad she hadn't spilled any of the liquid.

'She's a beautiful girl,' she murmured.

Pete nodded. 'Clever too.'

'You know her?'

'Vaguely. I had dealings with her father last time I was here. We did a good job for the government and he was delighted.'

'How come this new contract wasn't automatically given to you then?'

'It's too big to be awarded without competitive tenders being allowed. My spies tell me Morgan's offering rock-bottom prices.'

'Spies?' Sharon was amused. 'You have spies?'

'Not seriously.' Pete flashed her a smile. 'But a lot of information gets passed along the grape-vine, and if you keep your ears open when the delegates have had a few drinks ... Someone told me last night that Morgan's on to a new type of concrete that'll cut his costs by half. Naturally everyone wants to know what it is. If——' The wine waiter paused by their table and Pete broke off to consult with him.

He half-turned away from her as he did so, and Sharon was afforded a full view of Kane and Tassy. As always, the girl was exquisitely dressed, but tonight her usual discreet jewellery had been abandoned for a chunky gold necklace and long, swaying earrings which gave her an exotic air more normally associated with Thai bar girls. Which only went to show, Sharon thought cynically, that in every woman lies the harlot!

'Let's go over to the buffet before the crush,' she

suggested to Pete, pushing back her chair as soon as the wine waiter had left.

'Good idea.'

Pete followed her to the long table which ran the length of the far side of the pool. It was laden with colourful food: huge lobsters and prawns; tangy pork, lamb and beef, and enormous platters of rice and vegetables.

Plates piled high they returned to their table.

'Would you like to change places with me?' Pete asked.

'What for?'

'You won't see Morgan from *my* side.'

Heat rushed into Sharon's cheeks but she managed to keep her voice cool. 'What makes you think I mind seeing him?'

'Intuition. It's not a feminine prerogative!'

'It's not always accurate either!'

He chuckled and she forced herself to look Kane's way, determined to show Pete he was wrong. To her alarm Kane and Tassy rose and came towards them, but Kane walked past them to the buffet, pausing only to murmur a curt 'Good evening', though Tassy, surprisingly, stopped.

'Nice seeing you again Pete,' she purred. Jade-and-gold earrings swung wildly as she inclined her head, and a whiff of musky perfume wafted Sharon's way.

'It's good to see you, too,' Pete replied, rising. 'Do you know Miss Kingston?'

'We haven't actually met,' Tassy smiled at her. 'But I do remember seeing you before. In Bangkok, wasn't it?'

'Yes. I work for the Avonmore Group.'

'Of course.' Smiling at them both, the girl gracefully walked after Kane, and Pete sat down.

'Trust Morgan not to miss an opportunity,' he

grunted. 'Tassy has a helluva lot of influence with her father.'

'Then how come *you* aren't out with her tonight?'

'Because I wanted to be with you. I'm not a business machine like Morgan, you know. Now let's forget work and concentrate on ourselves. We're *much* nicer!'

Sharon made a determined effort to do as Pete suggested, and though she was only play-acting, she must have succeeded in convincing him, for he behaved as if she were the sole reason he had flown here from Japan. Yet even had this been the case, it would have raised no flutter in her pulse, for he no longer mattered to her. Indeed she was hard pressed to figure out why he ever had!

They were half-way through dinner when she saw Kane lead Tassy on to the dance floor. The way he held her suggested a deeper intimacy, and Sharon could hardly bear to watch them, remembering the last time—the only time—he had held *her* close. Thank heavens she hadn't given in to him; had refused to let passion rule her head. How demeaned she would now be feeling if she had! Yet her friends saw nothing wrong in sex without love; in going to bed with a man today, though they knew that come the morrow he would be intimate with someone else.

'It's stupid to marry without having experience of other men,' they said. 'You'll regret it.'

But she didn't, nor ever would. For her, sex without love was meaningless.

'Care to dance?' Pete broke into her thoughts, 'Or would you rather tell me what you were thinking about? You seemed miles away.'

'I was wondering why I can't treat sex lightly,' she said with a bluntness that took him by surprise. 'You think I'm stupidly old-fashioned don't you?'

'Well . . .' He paused. 'Let's say I think you're different from most of your contemporaries. But I wouldn't say I disagree with you.'

'That wasn't what you said a year ago.'

'A year ago I hadn't lived in Japan. But I've seen a whole new way of life there, and I like it.'

'The subservient virgin,' she teased. 'That's what *you* like!'

Frowning, he pushed back his chair, and she followed him on to the floor. The music was slow, the kind that did not invite intricacy of steps, but served rather as an excuse for restrained lovemaking. As Pete's arms came around her, Sharon had to resist the urge to push them away. With an effort she made herself relax, putting one arm round his neck and trying to act as if she were enjoying every minute of it. She did not glance Kane's way, but was painfully aware of him, his bronzed cheek pressed against the shining mass of Tassy's black hair, his tall, lean body moulded against her slender one. There was nothing virginal or innocent about Tassy's movements, she thought, and was sick with jealousy as she saw the red-tipped fingers caress the downbent head.

Sharon's nerves had reached breaking point when the music stopped, and before it could resume she hurried back to the table, pretending she wanted a dessert, though how she was going to force it down, she had no idea! In the event there was no problem, for she chose fruit salad, which she could push around her plate, while Pete was so preoccupied telling her about life in Japan, that she doubted he would have noticed if she had stuffed it into her shoes!

'Even though they believe in family tradition and heritage,' he concluded, 'it's a go-ahead country businesswise. Their industrial output is the best in the world, and so is the way they look after their employees.'

'Do you think you'll settle there?' she asked.

'I doubt it. The company want me to move around.'
He gave her a meaningful look. 'I may end up back in
London.'

Three months ago Sharon would have been over the
moon to hear this; now she could not care whether he
went to San Francisco or Timbuctoo! Given time,
maybe she would feel the same about Kane.

'Had enough?' Pete asked as he saw her set down
her spoon.

'Yes, thanks.'

She glanced at the dance floor, and seeing no sign of
Kane and Tassy, turned towards their table. With a
shock she saw the plates had been cleared away and
the waiter was busy laying a fresh cloth. She looked
towards the hotel, her eyes moving to the corner suite
at the top. The lights were on, and as she watched,
they dimmed and went out.

Oh Lord, she cried silently. How can I bear this
pain?

CHAPTER ELEVEN

DESPITE her late night, Sharon was up early next morning. Her sleep had been fraught with disturbing nightmares of Kane and Tassy, and it was a relief to wake up to bright sunshine pouring into her room.

Throwing back the sheet, she padded across to the window. A gentle breeze waved the palms and ruffled the surface of the pool, making it shimmer like a sapphire in its mosaic setting. The cleaners had already cleared away all signs of the party, and the serenity of the scene made her wonder if her memory was playing her false and last night had also been a dream.

The insistent buzz of the telephone made her turn from the window. It was the Head Housekeeper to say one of her assistants was ill and could Sharon supervise the maids on the top two floors. Fifty guests were arriving today, and their rooms had to be prepared.

Promising to see it was done, Sharon hurriedly dressed. She got on well with all the employees, and found them far more amenable than some of the staff she had dealt with in England. However, most of the maids were untrained and had little idea of what had to be done, and the instant she set foot on the top floor, one of them rushed over to tell her the refrigerators weren't working in the two suites in the West wing.

'Have you reported it to the engineer?' she asked.

'He's out,' the maid replied, 'and they don't know when he'll be back.'

Hiding her irritation, Sharon decided to look at the fridges herself, and was half-way along the corridor when she recollected Kane occupied one of the suites. Quickly she walked past it to the end one, and rang the buzzer.

Almost instantly, an irate American opened the door.

'What's kept you?' he scowled. 'I reported it an hour ago.'

'I only just got the message,' she apologised, following him into the lounge. 'What's the trouble?'

'It isn't making any ice.'

She opened the fridge door and peered at the control knobs, wondering if it had mistakenly been put on 'Defrost'. No, that wasn't it. She poked and prodded, switched the buttons on and off, and came to the conclusion it was an electrical fault.

'I'll get someone here as soon as possible,' she promised the disgruntled guest. 'Meanwhile I'll have a bucket of ice sent up.' She paused by the door. 'I think your neighbour's having the same trouble.'

'Maybe that's why he left his room early,' the American muttered. 'I heard his door slam before eight.'

'I'll check anyway,' Sharon said.

Heart pounding against her ribs, she went to the next room. Thank goodness Kane was out. She could take a peek at the refrigerator without his being any the wiser. To make sure he wasn't there, she pressed the buzzer, waited a few seconds, then pressed again. Still no answer. Taking the master key from her pocket, she turned the lock and went in.

The vast living room had not yet been tidied, and a brandy bottle and two glasses stood on the table beside the settee. Cushions were disarranged, and a crumpled shirt lay across a chair, where it had been flung, as if its owner had been too impatient to wait till he reached the bedroom. An image of Kane lying on the settee with Tassy came to torment her, and she almost ran to the little refrigerator that stood in the bar at the far end of the room.

A brief glance told her it was working perfectly, and she was half-way to the hall when she heard the bedroom door open. With a gasp she turned.

Kane stood on the threshold, his hair rumpled, his face flushed from sleep. Black silk pyjama trousers were tied loosely at his waist, but his chest was bare, showing shiny bronze skin, and a thick V of dark hair. Without a jacket, she saw that the width of his shoulders owed nothing to his tailor, and she hurriedly averted her eyes from the rippling muscles as he stretched tiredly.

'What the hell are you doing here?' he demanded.

'One of the m-maids said your fridge is out of order,' she stammered, 'I rang and got no reply, so I let myself in.'

'I was asleep. I didn't get to bed till four.'

'I'm sorry I disturbed you.' She still avoided looking at him. 'Anyway, I've checked it and it seems okay.'

'How did you get in?'

'I used the master key.'

He frowned. 'I'm not sure I like the idea of people wandering in and out uninvited. I've a lot of confidential papers here.'

'You should use the hotel safe,' Sharon replied.

'I have my own safe.' He yawned again, then looked apologetic. 'Sorry, but I'm still jet-lagged, and my late night didn't help any.'

'Obviously,' she said quietly.

His look was sharp. 'You're the one who's behaving obviously, Sharon.'

'Maybe it's infectious,' she retorted, and stalked out.

She was near to tears. No one seeing her and Kane together would have guessed how it had been with them in Bangkok. Was it because Tassy had come back on the scene, or because he had seen Pete kiss her? Either way, the result was the same.

Knowing work to be her best antidote, she remained supervising the chambermaids, and only after a late lunch at half-past three, did she shower and change and go into the village. The heat of the day had ebbed slightly, and she meandered through the old section, stopping to buy small items of copper and tin—the latter brightly polished to resemble silver—to take home as gifts.

She was returning to the taxi rank when her eye was caught by a dressmaker's shop. The shelves were piled with material in every colour and design, while at the back of the store five girls sat sewing, three at electric machines and two at the old-fashioned pedal type. A curtain at the far end parted, and a woman in loose-fitting black trousers and high-necked cotton jacket came out. Seeing Sharon, she glided forward, smiling.

'Yes?' she said in English. 'May I help you?' Her eyes were heavy-lidded, and her long black hair drawn back in a bun.

Sharon hesitated. The shop looked considerably more expensive than the one she had frequented until now, but there was no doubt the choice of material was better. Deciding to be extravagant, she stepped inside.

'I was wondering if you could make me something for evening?'

'In silk or cotton?'

'Cotton, please.'

The woman heaved down several bolts of fabric and placed them on the counter. There was such a profusion of choice, Sharon could not decide, but eventually whittled it down to a blue-and-yellow print, which she asked to see in the daylight.

The moment she did, she realised it was too garish for her, and shook her head. 'I think I'd better stick with something pastel.'

'Choosing a dress?' a deep voice enquired.

Even before she turned, Sharon knew it was Kane. It was their first encounter since she had gone into his suite, and he seemed a changed person, his expression almost friendly.

'I haven't decided on the material yet,' she said.

'You've come to the right place to find it, though. According to Tassy, Lala has the best selection.'

'Then she *must* be good.' Why did he have to bring Tassy into the conversation?

'I'm glad you vetoed the blue and yellow,' he went on. 'You need a smaller pattern.'

'I don't like small patterns. They make me feel like Kate Greenaway.'

'Never that—with your figure!' He stepped into the shop. 'What about those?' he asked, pointing to a shelf of fabric.

'They're pure silk,' Lala said, 'and madam wished for cotton.'

'What's wrong with silk?' Kane demanded, eyes probing Sharon's face.

'I don't want to spend that kind of money,' she said, furious at his lack of tact.

'Would you accept a length as a present?' he asked, then immediately added: 'Don't bother answering. I take back the question!'

Resisting the urge to hit him, Sharon turned away.

'I don't feel in the mood for looking at any more material,' she said to the dressmaker. 'I'll come back another time.'

'Sharon, don't go.' Kane's voice, authoritative and crisp, stopped her. 'I know you're annoyed with me, and I'm sorry, but don't let it spoil your afternoon. Please stay and choose something, and *I'll* go.'

'I have some lovely pink silk,' Lala intervened quickly. 'There are only a few metres left and I give you special price.'

Not giving Sharon a chance to say no, the woman brought out a small roll of shimmering silk and unwound a metre to hold against Sharon's body.

'Great,' Kane said. 'It goes with your colouring.'

Sharon pulled a face. 'Blondes in pink are too chocolate boxy.'

'It depends on the blonde.' His eyes narrowed appraisingly. 'Besides, your hair is honey gold and pink looks great on you. Take my word for it.'

'Why?'

'Because I've an eye for colour.'

'You're not short on conceit!'

'And you're not short of a sharp answer.'

'It's part of my charm.'

'You may be right—which means I must be a masochist!' Head to one side, he continued studying her. 'Let's choose a style for this and get out of here. I want to talk to you.'

Mutely, Sharon nodded. There was much she could read into what he had said, but she was scared of letting herself.

'How about this?' he asked, waving a pattern book at her.

With an effort she concentrated on the picture he was pointing to.

'The neckline's rather low,' she demurred.

'Why? You've beautiful breasts.'

'I don't need to show them to the world!'

'For once we're in agreement! So we'll get Lala to

raise the front a little. Apart from that, the design is perfect for you.'

Suddenly Sharon was struck by the humour of the situation. A few hours ago Kane had practically bitten her head off; now he was deciding how to dress her! If this was his way of making amends, she gave him full marks.

'Very well,' she said softly. 'I'll have the style *and* the material you like.'

Accepting his victory with a nonchalant shrug, he strolled out of the shop as measurements were taken. But he stayed near the entrance, clearly waiting, and Sharon kept check on her impatience as Lala jotted down all the figures and gave her a date for her first fitting.

'Any more shopping to do?' he asked as she finally joined him.

'Not with you! You've done enough persuading for one afternoon.'

'Then how about a swim? I've given myself the afternoon off. I worked all night with Mark.'

So he *hadn't* been with Tassy! Hiding her pleasure, Sharon followed him to a taxi, sitting silently in the corner as they careered out of the village.

'You seem to be on friendly terms with Wilburg,' he stated into the silence.

'I knew him in London.'

'Why didn't you tell me?'

'I didn't know *you* knew him.'

With a shrug Kane acknowledged the truth of this. 'Did you know he was coming here to bid for the contract?'

'No. I haven't seen or heard from him since he went to Japan nearly a year ago.'

There was another silence, and Sharon looked at

Kane from the corner of her eyes. But his expression was impassive.

'I apologise for my off-handedness at dinner last night,' he said abruptly. 'Also for my temper when you came to check the refrigerator.'

'Apology accepted,' she said airily, as if his attitude had not bothered her. 'I expect you're on edge about the contract.'

'That had nothing to do with it.'

Sharon did not pursue the subject, and neither did he until the taxi stopped to let them out.

'I'd like to talk to you alone,' he said as he paid off the driver. 'Let's find somewhere quiet.'

'I thought you wanted to swim?'

'I want to settle things between us first. There's——' he broke off as Pete suddenly came towards them and put his arm round Sharon's shoulder.

'What happened to you, honey?' he demanded. 'You promised to come with me to the Islands.'

'I never said any such thing,' Sharon protested.

'We arranged it last night when we were having a nightcap,' Pete insisted, and glanced at Kane. 'Sorry to barge in on you like this, but Sharon and I——'

'I was going to my room anyway,' Kane cut in, and with a cool nod to both of them, turned on his heel.

'What on earth are you playing at?' Sharon rounded on Pete the instant they were alone. 'You know we didn't make any arrangements for today!'

'I thought you'd like to make Morgan jealous.'

'If I did, I'd have told you,' she cried furiously. 'When I need your help I'll ask for it.' She went to push past him but he stayed her with his hand.

'I'm sorry, Sharon. I wouldn't upset you for the world.'

'Well, you have,' she retorted. 'It was a stupid thing to do.' Pushing his hand away, she stormed up to her room.

Once there, she flopped into a chair. Pete had a nerve! If he was so concerned about her happiness, how come he had gone to Japan and never contacted her again? Yet his attitude was of no importance compared with Kane's. *He* had behaved like a jealous lover from the minute he had arrived in Pattaya and seen her lying on a sun mattress next to Pete!

Although he had feigned indifference when she had telephoned him immediately afterwards, she now realised he had been putting on an act. And a man wasn't jealous of a woman unless he felt something for her. It was a wonderful thought, and her despondency lifted. Of course his feelings could merely be sexual, but as he had also intimated he enjoyed being with her and appreciated her intelligence, surely that was a step in the right direction?

Happily she changed into a fresh cotton dress before going downstairs. Quite irrationally she suddenly felt she had a future with Kane. All she had to do was make him see it too!

CHAPTER TWELVE

SHARON reached the foyer to hear that the fifty guests had arrived and were satisfied with their accommodation. Things seemed to be going well all round! She went in search of Kane but he was nowhere to be seen, and she decided not to beard him in his room. Some things should be taken slowly, and the taming of Kane was one of them!

To help pass the time, she rearranged the flowers in the main reception areas, a task of joy when there were such wonderful blooms to hand, and she was still feeling uplifted when she returned to her room to change for the evening.

Determined to bowl Kane over, she chose one of her most sophisticated dresses, a simple black shift with narrow diamanté straps holding up a minimal bodice. It showed every curve of her body: the full, firm breasts, handspan waist and rounded hips. To enhance the picture of sophisticated abandon, she brushed her hair into a cascade of curls that lay on her shoulders like molten foam, and was putting on a second coat of mascara when there was a tap on the door.

Getting no response to her 'come in', she went to open it. To her surprise Pete stood on the threshold, a cellophane box in his hand.

'A peace offering,' he said sheepishly, holding out a spray of orchids.

'Thank you.' She lifted the lid and lightly touched their fragile petals. 'They're beautiful.'

'Not as beautiful as you.' He edged into the room. 'I

behaved very badly today and I want you to know I'm sorry.'

'Forget it. You're forgiven.' She looked at the flowers again, then chuckled. 'They're lovely and it's sweet of you to give me them, but I don't think I've enough dress to pin them on!'

'I'm delighted to agree,' he grinned. 'Put them in a vase instead.'

He watched as she did, his expression unusually serious.

'Anything wrong?' she asked.

'No. Just thinking how lovely you are. Not just outside, Sharon—but inside too.'

'That's an even nicer gift than your flowers!'

He moved closer. 'If you don't have any other plans, how about dinner?' He saw her hesitation. 'A drink then?'

Why not? she thought, and nodded. It was only eight and Kane might not be down for ages. Together she and Pete walked down the corridor.

'How did the conference go today?' she asked.

'A total waste. Morgan did the right thing staying away.'

'Why? What happened?'

'Bonlam's still keeping us dangling. He said something about the Prime Minister being away for two weeks, but I reckon it's a stall. I've half a mind to pull out.'

'I thought you had a good chance?'

'We do,' Pete said without enthusiasm, and stepped with her into the elevator.

Sharon's colour rose high as she saw Kane standing there. He glanced at Pete's hand on her arm, his expression indicative of his belief that she and Pete had just come from her room.

Well they had, but it wasn't as he thought! Yet she

knew he had already judged and condemned her. Cursing the Fate that had made him be in this elevator at this particular moment, she stared silently at the wall. The instant they reached the lobby he strode out without a word or glance, and Pete raised his eyebrows at her.

'You know what he suspects, don't you?'

'Yes.'

'You want me to go and straighten him out?'

'Why bother?' she shrugged, watching from the corner of her eye as Kane greeted Tassy. Had he arranged to dine with the girl before he had tried to make amends with herself, or had he called after Pete's stupid behaviour this afternoon? She would have given a great deal to know.

'Sure you won't change your mind and have dinner with me tonight?' Pete asked, guiding her across to the Beachcomber bar.

'Maybe I will,' she said with a bright smile. 'It's a lady's prerogative to change her mind.'

'Especially a liberated one!'

She laughed and perched on a bar stool, hoping Kane and Tassy wouldn't come in here, too. She knew she was behaving like a lovesick schoolgirl but could not help herself. If only that damned contract was decided and Kane could fly out of her life. She could never rebuild it while he was here.

'Have you, Sharon?' Pete asked.

With a start she realised he had been talking to her. 'Sorry, Pete, I was miles away.'

'I just wanted to know if you've really forgiven me for this afternoon?'

'Of course I have.'

'Then how come you're mentally miles away, instead of being over the moon sitting next to me!'

'I can't get really close to you,' she drawled, 'your head's too swollen!'

He burst out laughing. 'I walked into that, didn't I? But apart from a swelled head, I'm attentive, loving, and willing to take no for an answer!'

'An ideal boyfriend,' she joked.

'An ideal husband too, when the time comes.' His expression grew serious. 'And I think it's coming due now.'

'I doubt that,' she commented flatly. 'The work ethos is too important to you, Pete. Even married, you'd still treat your home as a hotel and your wife as an ornament to pick up and put down as it pleases you.'

'It might please *her* too! I'd pay the bills and make sure she's sexually happy.'

'How would you know when you'd be away so much? Anyway, most women want more than sex today. They want to be part of their husband's life. If——'

She forced herself to stop, reluctant to repeat what she had already told him in England. Besides, it was a waste of time. Pete would never change. And even if he did, she didn't want him.

He sipped his whisky and stared at her thoughtfully. 'I know you think me a dyed-in-the-wool chauvinist, but I'm genuinely ready to prove you wrong if you'd give me a chance.'

But Sharon was no longer listening, her attention given to Kane and Tassy, who had just come in. How elegant the girl looked in a white dress that offset her olive skin. She moved languidly across the room, dark eyes glowing as she gave all her attention to the man beside her. But as she neared the end of the bar where Pete and Sharon were sitting, she looked across at them and smiled. Then horror of horrors, she glided over, followed by an obviously reluctant Kane.

'I hope my father didn't give you too hard a time this afternoon, Pete?' she asked.

'No more than he gave anyone else. But how much longer will we have to wait for an answer?'

'How would I know?' she pouted.

'I bet you know everything.'

Tassy gave a soft laugh. 'My father never listens to me. But I promise I'll tell him how you feel.'

'Me, and all the *other* guys here,' Pete retorted, in no way appeased.

'Oh dear, you really *are* cross.' She glanced at Kane, whose expression was making it clear he wished to move on. 'Why don't we join forces and eat together? Then I can try to appease two companies in the same evening!'

Kane's dark blue eyes rested fleetingly on Sharon. 'Why not?' he shrugged, as if it was of no importance who joined them.

Pete gave Sharon a questioning look, and though the last thing she wanted was to dine with Kane and Tassy, she had no intention of letting them know it.

'Suits me,' she said gaily, and clasped Pete's arm as they left the bar and wended their way to a table by the pool.

Tassy conferred at length with the maître, then announced she had chosen a special Thai dinner for them all.

'Nothing too spicy or hot,' she promised, 'so you needn't ask for glasses of milk to cool your throats!'

She was as good as her word, for the food, when it came, was subtly flavoured, and had obviously been specially prepared. Predictably, the highway contract dominated the conversation, and though Pete and Kane appeared to speak quite openly about it, Sharon detected an underlying reticence on both their parts.

The surprise came when Kane referred to 'our own special concrete', and she intercepted a momentary glance between Tassy and Pete. She could have sworn it was a silent exchange, as if the two had far greater knowledge of each other than they admitted, and she wondered if they had met when Pete was last here. Yet surely he would have mentioned it? Indeed, he had gone out of his way to tell her they had never met. Even as she pondered this, Tassy started talking about her years in the States, and Sharon, working out dates, realised the woman had been in America while Pete was in Bangkok.

Tassy and Pete started swapping stories about their experiences at Harvard, and Sharon eyed Kane, willing him to ask her to dance. But the eyes that met hers were cold as icebergs, and when he did finally push back his chair, it was to interrupt Tassy's conversation with Pete.

Cut off in mid-flow, Pete led Sharon on to the floor too. He held her lightly as he skilfully manoeuvred them through the crowded dancers, and happening to glance up, she saw his eyes fixed on the Thai girl.

'Tassy's very beautiful,' she murmured.

'No more so than you,' he smiled, drawing her close and resting his chin on her head.

She tried to stop herself wishing it was Kane's arms around her, but she could think of nothing else, and she was searching for an excuse to return to their table when she saw their waiter wheel a trolley towards it.

'Looks like we've more to eat,' she said brightly. 'Let's go back.'

They reached their table almost at the same moment as Kane and Tassy, and Pete looked at the spirit lamp and frying pan set out on the trolley and raised his eyebrows at the Thai girl.

'If my eyes don't deceive me,' he grinned, 'we're having Crêpes Suzette!'

'Right, first time.'

'What's with your promise of a totally Thai dinner?' he teased.

'Desserts aren't our forte,' she confessed, 'so I compromised. But we can have them with chilli peppers instead of orange if you'd prefer!'

'I'll take them Suzette's way!'

Tassy laughed, head flung back. It was the first genuinely carefree gesture Sharon had seen her make, and it robbed her of her usual masklike grace and calm. She really was a beautiful girl. No wonder Kane found her desirable.

The crêpes—smelling of oranges and brandy—were flamed and set before them, and the maître waited for their approval, which they all gave unstintingly.

'Best I've had outside of Paris,' Pete announced.

'I endorse that,' Kane agreed, 'though not the Paris part. Best French cooking I've ever tasted was in Saigon.'

The maître looked delighted. 'At Maison Charles?'

'You know it?'

'I worked there before coming here. And you're right, sir. It's superb.'

'I can take you to one equally as good in Bangkok,' Tassy interpolated. 'Once these boring negotiations are over, we'll have a celebration dinner there.'

'Boring?' Kane questioned sardonically. 'You know you enjoy watching us bid against each other. It gives you a thrill to see the in-fighting, the haggling.'

A flash of irritation—so quick as to be gone almost before it had registered—passed over Tassy's face. 'What a mean thing to say!' she pouted. 'Nothing will please me more than to have the whole thing over— even though it means you'll be leaving us.' She looked intently into Kane's face, uncaring that her emotion was clearly visible. 'I never thought you'd need me to *tell* you that.'

'Didn't you?' Kane said softly. 'Don't you know how difficult you are to read?'

'You haven't tried hard enough, then.' She lightly touched his hand with her slim brown fingers, and Sharon quickly looked away.

'Care to dance?' Pete said suddenly, and Sharon was about to rise when she realised he was looking at Tassy.

Giving Kane's hand a final, lingering touch, the girl rose, leaving Sharon and Kane alone. He made no effort to speak, his eyes watching the couples on the floor, his hands inert on the table, as if he were totally relaxed. Yet his tall, lithe body held a tension that denied this, as did his mouth, which was so tightly set that the lines either side of it were deeply indented.

'How about joining them?' he asked indifferently.

Thinking it would be better to dance with him than sit together in frozen silence, she nodded. But the instant his arms came around her she knew she had made the wrong decision. His nearness set her aflame, and breathing in the warmth of him made her limbs turn to jelly.

'Relax,' he ordered. 'I'm not going to rape you!'

'That's a relief to know.'

'A relief for you, but a darned strain for me,' he said unexpectedly.

She was so startled she missed a step. 'Is that meant as a compliment?'

'A statement of fact,' he said flatly. 'You do unexpected things to me, Sharon.'

'I'm sorry,' she said sweetly.

'So am I. Usually I can control my sexual urges.' His voice roughened. 'You think I want to feel like this about you? You're a bloody tease, Sharon Kingston, and a clever, ambitious young woman into the bargain. Certainly not the sort I——'

'Stop it!' she cried swiftly. 'I'm not interested in your opinion of me.' She tried to pull free of him but his grip tightened, one arm clasping her waist like a vice, the other grasping her shoulder. 'Let go of me,' she hissed.

'No. Not till I'm ready.'

The implacability of his voice told her he had no intention of doing as she asked, and knowing that to struggle further might result in an unpleasant scene, she gave in. For several moments they danced in silence.

'Well,' he said tightly, 'aren't you going to say anything?'

'About what?'

'My opinion of you.'

'It's such a rigid one,' she said tonelessly, 'I'd never be able to change it.'

'At least you should try. Come on, Sharon, where's your spirit?'

She tilted her head to look into his face. His expression told her he was in the mood to enjoy a show of strength, and she determined not to encourage him. Besides, she would die rather than let him know how much his assessement of her had hurt.

'I don't believe in pointless argument, Kane. You're a man of strong views, and if you think I'm—if you have a particular idea of me, then so be it. I couldn't care less what you think of me. You're not part of my life and never will be.'

'Well, that's a bit of spirit anyway,' he replied, a smile on his mouth, though not in his eyes.

She made no answer, and silently they danced. His hold on her was looser, but even as she tried to ease away, his fingers tightened. Giving in to the inevitable, and anxious not to allow the sensual beat of the music to make her more aware of Kane's body than she already was, she forced herself to talk, steering for the one subject she knew would take his mind off her.

'I was surprised to hear you talk about the new concrete you've developed. I thought you kept things like that a secret?'

'Not at this stage. All our rivals know we have it. What they don't know is how to make it.'

'How long can you keep the formula to yourself? Sooner or later someone will find out how to copy it.'

'They won't need to. We intend patenting our discovery and granting licences to anyone who wants to use it. But as of now, the secret is ours and will cut our costings for *this* particular contract by a—well let's say a substantial amount.'

'Which makes you certain to win?'

'Yes.'

'So why——'

'Shush,' he ordered as the tempo of the music changed. 'Stop talking business and concentrate on *me*.'

'I thought you didn't like ambitious, clever teases?'

'I love them—on a temporary basis.'

'I'm not a temp, Kane.'

'Pity. We could have fun.'

'So you said in Bangkok. And in case you've forgotten, my answer was no—and still is.'

'Pity,' he repeated.

His breath was warm on her ear and she could not suppress a shiver of desire.

'You want me,' he went on huskily. 'Don't bother denying it.'

'I'm not denying it. But it's a sexual response, nothing more.'

'I don't want any more. Sex is quite enough.'

'I prefer it with love,' she said stonily.

'Shows how young you are,' he chided.

The music stopped and he paused, waiting for it to resume. The floor was packed and they were hemmed in by other couples, making it impossible for Sharon to dart away from him. On the far rim of the floor she glimpsed Pete. He seemed to be listening intently to what Tassy was saying—something important, if her expression was anything to go by—and once again she wondered if they knew each other better than they admitted.

The music started again, a slow languorous beat that fired her blood; Kane's too it seemed, for he rested his hands upon the small of her back and pressed the lower half of her body tightly against his. She felt his arousal, as she knew he meant her to, and could not suppress the tremor that rippled through her thighs.

'You *do* want me,' he said thickly. 'You're a sexy little bitch, Sharon. Or doesn't Pete satisfy you?'

Fury engulfed her, killing passion dead, and regardless of people around them, she tore from his hold and pushed her way back to the table. Kane followed hard on her heels, holding out her chair for her so solicitously it was impossible to guess how insulting he had just been. With shaking hands she went to open her bag for her handkerchief, and was surprised to find the catch undone. She closed it, then deliberately gave her attention to the dancers, knowing if she tried to speak to Kane, she would burst into tears.

'Don't look so bereft,' he bit out suddenly. 'Tassy loves flirting, but it doesn't mean a thing.'

Blankly Sharon looked round at him, and seeing his glittering eyes move from her to the dance floor, realised that he thought her distress was caused by seeing Pete and Tassy dancing cheek to cheek.

'I couldn't care less what Pete does,' she said stiltedly. 'He means nothing to me.'

'Is that why you entertained him in your room earlier this evening?'

'I entertained him for five minutes!' she flared, temper making her forget she had vowed not to defend herself. 'He came to bring me some flowers—for no other reason. So put your salacious thoughts in the trashcan!'

'And what were the flowers for?' Kane demanded. 'For services rendered?'

'Oh, you're a hateful swine!' Fury rose like a tidal wave. 'Just to satisfy your morbid curiosity about my private life, Mr Morgan, he merely brought them as an apology for this afternoon.'

'I'd have thought you owed *him* the apology. You were the one who forgot you had a date.'

'I didn't forget.'

Having said as much as she had, she decided she might as well set the record straight. Let Kane ignore her from now on if he wished, but there was no reason for him to think her a tease.

'Pete pretended we had, because he thought I wanted to make you——' Heavens, she daren't use the word 'jealous' or Kane would guess how she felt about him—'because he thought you were on the make and he wanted to protect me from you.'

There was a tense silence and before Kane could reply, Pete and Tassy rejoined them. Unable to bear any more false bonhomie, Sharon glanced at her watch and stood up.

'Afraid you'll have to excuse me, folks. We've a cruise group arriving at midnight and I have to settle them in.'

'You certainly work unsocial hours,' Pete grumbled.

'It's part of the job—and I love it. No, don't come with me,' she said as he went to rise. 'I'll be too busy to talk to you, anyway.'

Before he could protest, she hurried away, head high, body moving seductively beneath the soft silk of her dress. Only when she was out of their sight did her step falter, and she momentarily gave way to the misery caused by Kane's wounding remarks. He professed himself a good judge of character, yet he was way off beam in his assessment of hers. Unless he was deliberately blinding himself, unwilling to see her as she was in case he fell in love with her? It was a startling thought, and she instantly rejected it. Love did not come into his calculations. All he wanted was sex and momentary gratification.

Pushing him from her mind, she went to her room to change into a denim skirt and blouse, then down to the lobby to greet the new arrivals. It was an hour before everyone was settled, and the last couple she saw to their suite invited her to join them for a coffee. Too strung up to sleep, she accepted, and they regaled her with details of their cruise and a glimpse of some of the lovely things they had bought en route.

It was nearly two o'clock before she left them. The corridor was deserted as she walked to the elevator, though music and voices could be faintly heard coming from some of the rooms. This was the second time in a matter of days she had been on Kane's floor, and she quickened her step. She reached the elevator and pressed the bell, then knowing she had a moment to wait, moved to the table opposite to break off some sagging blooms from the display of flowers that stood in it. As she did, she glimpsed a flash of white as Tassy emerged from Kane's suite.

Half-hidden by the foliage, Sharon knew the girl had not seen her, and she braced herself, wondering how to react when Tassy reached her side. But surprisingly the girl went in the opposite direction and disappeared through the service door. Talk about discretion! She obviously preferred walking down ten flights to being seen entering the elevator from a specific floor! Yet Sharon's amusement was tinged with bitterness that Kane should look down his nose at her because he thought she was having an affair with Pete, when he himself was doing exactly the same with Tassy. Or didn't he believe that what was sauce for the goose was also sauce for the gander?

In her room she undressed and went to bed, even though she knew she was still too het up to sleep. It was a good thing she had seen Tassy just now, for it had at last put paid to the dreams she had foolishly continued to cherish deep in her heart, even when her head had told her how hopeless they were of materialising. Tassy and Kane. Yet if not Tassy it would be another girl. A man like Kane would never find a shortage of bed companions; and since that was all he wanted . . .

'I hate you, Kane Morgan!' she muttered into her pillow, and as the tears came, hopelessly admitted she did not mean a word of it.

CHAPTER THIRTEEN

THE following day Bud Cameron returned, and was full of praise for the way Sharon had handled the various problems that had arisen during his absence.

'Things aren't usually as frenetic as this,' he assured her. 'But what with the cruise passengers arriving and all the building contractors here, our staff are stretched to capacity.'

'It doesn't do staff any harm to work flat out on occasion,' she said. 'It keeps them on their toes.'

'Some have been on their toes so long, they feel like ballet dancers!' Bud Cameron ran his hand through his hair, making the sandy strands stand on end. 'Still, I think the pressure will soon be easing. On my way in just now, I saw all the executives heading for taxis, and I overheard one of them saying they'd been called to Bonlam's house for a final meeting.'

Sharon was delighted. With luck, Kane would soon be out of her hair and she could get on with the business of living. The business of loving was a thing of the past, she vowed. Twice bitten would make her ten times shy!

Frequently during the rest of the day she kept looking to see if any of the men were back, but it was well after five before a fleet of taxis deposited them at the main entrance. Everyone was so grim-faced as they trooped into the lobby that she had no need to ask if they had fared well, and when most of them asked for their bills to be prepared, she knew the Minister's decision had indeed been made.

Deliberately Sharon loitered in the Reception area,

telling herself she was only there in case she was needed, yet knowing she was prompted by curiosity to know as soon as possible which company had won the lucrative contract.

The sight of Pete, grinning from ear to ear as he walked in with his entourage of Japanese, gave her the answer, and though pleased for him, she could not help a momentary pang of disappointment for Kane—which showed what a fool she was!

'We've won,' Pete cried exuberantly, catching her by the arms. 'Our costs were lower than anyone else's, can you believe? You must help me celebrate, sweetheart. I've got to call Tokyo first, but I'll be right back.'

Sharon had little time to ponder on what had happened, for a new cruise group were arriving within the hour, and she had to ensure that the tours they had booked through the hotel were all in order. Nonetheless, her mind wandered frequently to Kane, and how he must be feeling. He had been so positive his new concrete would cut his costs sufficiently to make it impossible for anyone to compete against him, that he must be bitterly disappointed to be proved wrong.

'You're wanted at Reception, Miss Kingston.'

A bell boy was at her elbow with the message, and she hurried back to the front desk. To her surprise Kane was waiting for her there, his expression black as thunder.

'I want to speak to you privately,' he said abruptly.

'I'm busy.'

'I don't care if you're entertaining the Queen! I mean right now.'

Because he looked ready to make a scene, regardless, Sharon led him into the small office that had been allocated to her. She sat behind the desk and motioned

Kane to a chair. But he ignored it and stood facing her, his eyes blazing.

'What were you doing in my suite last night?' he demanded.

'What?' She could not believe she had heard correctly.

'You heard me. What were you doing in my suite?'

'I don't know what you're talking about.'

'Don't give me that,' he shouted. 'Who else has a master key to all the rooms?'

'Mr Cameron, the manager. But no one else.'

'Well, I'll absolve *him*,' Kane retorted. 'but not *you*. Someone got at my papers last night, but I didn't notice it until this morning, as I was preparing to leave for the meeting.'

'And you think it was me?' She was incredulous.

'Damn right I do! The whole file was rifled through, and the formula for the concrete—which was in a locked deed box—had been prised open.' He leaned across the desk, his hands planted either side of her, so that she could not rise. 'Bonlam just told me the Japanese costs were five per cent lower than ours, because they'll be using a special concrete which Wilburg has formulated.'

Kane's face lowered to hers, and Sharon saw a nerve beating frantically in his temple.

'Do you hear that, you thieving bitch?' he thundered. 'Wilburg couldn't formulate a chocolate eclair! So he got you to steal *my* formula!'

The blood rushed to Sharon's face and rage, equal to Kane's, tore through her. 'Are you seriously saying I sneaked into your room and stole the specifications?'

'That's it exactly! So quit acting the innocent. If I could prove what you did, I'd have you behind bars! My only consolation is that you and Wilburg deserve one another!'

'And you deserve having your ideas stolen! How could you be stupid enough to leave them in your hotel bedroom!'

'They were in my wall safe,' Kane snapped. 'I took them out at midnight to glance through them, and left them in my desk because I wasn't going to leave my room any more.'

Nor his bed either, she thought grimly, remembering Tassy coming from his suite at two o'clock that very morning. Anguish swamped her rage and momentarily she was too overcome to speak. Not that it would have done her any good, for Kane was still ranting on, his skin ashen beneath its tan.

'I never went anywhere near your room last night!' she stated, cutting across him. 'Ever since you came to Pattaya you've behaved like a madman with me. One minute you're friendly, the next I'm top of your hit list! Well, I won't stand for it any longer. Unless you retract your accusation I'll ask the Avonmore Group for legal advice. I'm not a thief and I won't allow you to call me one!'

For answer, Kane swung on his heel and stormed out, the furniture trembling as he crashed the door shut.

Shakily, Sharon leaned back in her chair. Her anger against Kane abated as quickly as it had risen, for she understood exactly how he felt. Months of negotiations wasted and thousands of pounds lost. It was an expensive business to prepare detailed specifications for such a massive project, and to lose out because one of your rivals has stolen the very invention on which you based your entire quote . . .

Thoughtfully she went over everything Kane had said. She knew she wasn't guilty, so it had to be someone else. And that raised a whole host of questions.

Unable to bear her own company, she left her office, almost knocking into Pete, who was heading towards it.

'I was coming in search of you,' he said. 'I thought you'd like to help me celebrate.' He noticed her expression. 'You look as if you've lost a dollar and found a cent.'

'I feel like it. I've just had an awful scene with Kane.'

'I bet he's in a foul mood,' Pete grinned. 'He thought he had the contract sewn up. Still, he has no business taking it out on you.'

'It was more than a bad mood. He accused me of stealing his new formula and giving it to you.'

'*What?*' Pete lost his smile. 'The guy's crazy!'

'Crazy or not, he believes I went to his room and looked through his papers.'

'Well . . .' Pete seemed lost for words. 'I must say that's a novel approach,' he said finally. 'Accuse your rival of cheating instead of admitting you lost out because you quoted too high. We underbid him and he's obviously a lousy loser!'

'No, Pete, it's more than that. He said you were only able to cut your costs because you announced you had a new concrete.'

'So we have. Construction companies are always searching for ways to strengthen building materials. Our formula may be similar to his, but no more than that. And as for accusing *you* . . . Do you want me to go and hit him?'

'That's the *last* thing I want.'

'At least let me talk to him.'

'I'd rather you didn't.' To have two guests at the Avonmore fight over her—which was what would happen—would do nothing to enhance her reputation with the Group. 'It's best to forget the whole thing,

Pete. As you say, he's feeling sore and will hit out at anyone he can. I'll—I'll try to forget the whole thing.'

'I still think you should let me go and talk to him.' Pete stopped as he saw her expression. 'Very well, have it your way. But come and have a drink. You deserve it.'

Meekly she went with him to the bar, and after a champagne cocktail felt better able to cope with the tumultuous emotions Kane's accusations had aroused. She could not understand why he should make a scapegoat out of her instead of doing the rational thing and reporting the matter to the management. Unless he enjoyed believing the worst of her!

Vaguely she heard Pete talking about his future. He was returning to Japan for a while, but would then be coming back to Thailand.

'I hope you'll still be here,' he said.

'I've a six-month contract. But I may ask to go home earlier.' Her voice trailed away and she averted her head, unwilling for him to see the tears that had rushed into her eyes.

'Hey there.' Pete gently turned her chin. 'You're not worrying about what Kane said, are you?'

'I can't help it. No one likes being accused of dishonesty.'

'If it comes to it,' Pete said grimly, 'I could accuse him of stealing *our* formula! As I said, they're remarkably similar!'

'Then why did you ask me if I knew anything about *his*?'

Pete looked taken aback. 'Did I?'

'Yes. Don't you remember?'

'Can't say I do. I think you misunderstood me—or else I put it badly. What I meant was that we'd developed a new mix, and I wondered how close in concept it was, to Kane's.'

Though not completely satisfied with this answer, Sharon did not argue. She had been so alert to Kane's position, so defensive about him, she could well have misinterpreted what Pete had said.

'Maybe you've been spying on each other,' she said wryly. 'Most big companies do, if they get the chance!'

'You'd make a beautiful spy, darling,' he smiled. 'Let me know when you want to apply for the job!'

'I like my present one too much. Which reminds me, I'm still on duty. Thanks for the drink, Pete.'

'See you later?'

She nodded, reluctant to commit herself, and returned to the Front Desk, where she was kept busy until early evening, dealing with new arrivals.

After a cool shower, she took a taxi to the village. It had been a traumatic day and she found it relaxing to wander around the little shops and see the smiling Thai women, who by this time recognised her and shyly tried out their English on her—while she reciprocated with her hard-learned Thai! Eventually she found herself outside Lala's shop. The dressmaker was in the window, putting a dress on display, and she saw Sharon and waved.

'You've come to try on your dress?' she asked.

'Is it ready for a fitting then?' She was not in the mood, but did not wish to appear rude.

Lala nodded and Sharon followed her into a cubicle and tried on the half-finished silk dress she had chosen with Kane. He was right about pink suiting her. It gave her skin the lustre of a pearl. Yet she doubted she would ever wear the dress, for it would serve only to remind her of a man she had to forget.

She was turning to leave when she noticed a piece of embroidered white brocade on the counter.

'That was woven especially for Miss Bonlam,' Lala said, seeing her eye it.

'It's beautiful.' Sharon traced the gold threads with her finger. 'She wore it the other night when we had dinner together.'

'Ah, yes. I forgot you knew her. You will be seeing her again this evening, maybe?'

'I'm not sure. Why?'

'If you do, can you give her this?' Lala reached behind the counter and lifted out a key. 'Miss Bonlam's maid brought in the dress this morning to have a pocket mended, and we found it in the hem.'

Incredulously Sharon looked at the heavy brass key. It was an exact facsimile of the master key for the top four floors of the hotel!

With trembling hands she opened her bag to see if hers was on the bunch, then recollected she had left it in the safe in her office.

'You say this was found in the hem of Miss Bonlam's dress?' she asked, to make sure she had heard correctly.

'Yes, Teri—the seamstress who found it—called me over to show me. There was a small hole in the pocket and I think the key must have slipped through the lining and settled in the hem. All my dresses are fully lined in pure silk,' Lala explained, 'so the key wouldn't have fallen on the floor.'

'Does Miss Buntam know you've found it?' Sharon asked.

"Not yet. I called her this morning, but she was out.'

Sharon picked up the key and studied it again. It could not belong to the Avonmore. She was letting her imagination run away with her. Nevertheless, she had a strong inclination to check it against the one on her bunch.

'I'll take it with me and see Miss Bonlam gets it,' she informed Lala. 'If she calls you in the meantime, tell her I have it.'

Still perplexed, Sharon left the shop. She had lost all further desire to wander round the village, and spotting a taxi cruising by, she hailed it.

If this key was identical to her own it would open up a whole new avenue of suspicion; one that could lead to the downfall of several important people. It was an exhilarating, yet frightening thought.

CHAPTER FOURTEEN

THE ride in the taxi helped Sharon calm down, and the calmer she became, the greater grew her certainty that the key now in her possession was one of the hotel's master keys. But why had Tassy had it? Logically there were two reasons. The girl was either in league with Kane to get into Pete's room by herself and look through his files, or with Pete to get sight of Kane's!

Yet had Tassy wanted to go through Kane's files, surely she could have done so during her frequent visits to his suite? There must have been many occasions when he had left her alone in the sitting room. Of course if she had wanted to photograph the documents she would have needed more time, as well as the safety of knowing she was not going to be disturbed. Hence the key.

On the other hand, Tassy could be in league with Kane to spy on Pete. Which meant Kane's accusation against herself had been an act to cover his own wrongdoing. Somehow it seemed out of character for him, and though aware her feelings for him were colouring her judgment, she could not dismiss the thought that he was basically too forthright to stoop to spying.

The more she considered it, the deeper grew her conviction that the man Tassy was in league with, was Pete.

But how had the girl got hold of the key in the first place? Sharon had no need to search for the answer. The other night, when she had returned to her table after dancing with Kane, she had found her bag unclasped. At the time she had not given it a thought, but now she realised that Tassy or Pete, dancing past their unoccupied table, had filched the key from it.

The taxi stopped outside the hotel and Sharon rushed to her office and unlocked her wall safe. The keys were all there! But no, one was missing! So she was right. It *had* been taken from her purse last night.

Without a moment's hesitation she dialled Kane's suite. There was no answer, and she left word at Reception for them to locate him.

'When you do, please say I wish to speak to him urgently,' she said. 'I'll be in the hotel all evening.'

She returned to her room and for the next hour paced the floor. At last, unable to bear the waiting, she decided to see if he was having dinner on the terrace. She was at the door when the phone rang and she rushed to answer it. But it was Pete, saying he was leaving tomorrow and hoped he could have a farewell drink with her.

'I know you're always pleading work,' he added, 'but at least come and say goodbye.'

Seeing him now was the last thing Sharon wanted. 'May we make it later?' she hedged, praying she would soon be hearing from Kane. 'Say nine-thirty?'

'Sure. I'll meet you in the bar.'

Going down to the ground floor, Sharon wondered what she should say to Pete if she had not managed to see Kane beforehand. But there was still two hours to go, and he was certain to return to the hotel before then.

To make sure he had not walked past Reception without being seen, she went into all the public rooms. No sign of him anywhere. Nor was he having an early dinner on the terrace. Despondently she sat at a table and ordered a snack. This was as good a vantage point as any to wait for Kane.

But even though she ate slowly, he had still not put in an appearance by the time she had finished. Could he have left for London already? But surely Reception would have told her if he had checked out. Unless he had left Mr Victorsen to pay his bill! It had not occurred to her until now, and she pushed back her chair and rushed to the cashier's desk.

'No one's asked for Mr Morgan's bill,' she was assured, 'but if anyone does, we'll let you know.'

Dejectedly she wandered to the bookstall and examined the titles. Half-an-hour dragged by and she went to a house phone and dialled Kane's suite again. Still no reply. Knowing she could no longer delay meeting Pete, she went to the bar.

It was almost deserted; quite a different picture from last night, when it had been filled with hard-nosed contractors waiting to see if *their* bid was going to be the lucky one. Now the decision was made and they were all packing to leave. Indeed some had already gone.

Pete rose to greet her and she found it hard to look him in the face, though as he guided her to a table and gave their order, he appeared so normal she began to doubt the validity of her suspicions. In beige slacks and cream knit shirt, his blond hair streaked silver by the sun, he was every girl's dream of the virile male. But not her, she thought happily. That day was long gone.

'I'm off first thing in the morning,' he said, raising his brandy to her in a silent salute.

'You must be over the moon the way things have worked out for you,' she forced herself to say.

'I am,' he agreed. 'But *you* don't look it. I'd like to think it's because I'm leaving,' he went on softly.

What gall he had after the way he had left her last year! With an effort she refrained from saying so.

'I'm disappointed you won't be around to see my new dress,' she lied, and in that moment determined to put her half-formed suspicions to the test. After all, she had nothing to lose. If he took offence, who cared? He was unlikely to report her to Bud Cameron.

'Save it for my return and we'll go out and celebrate,' he said.

'Will we?' She set down her drink and clasped her hands in her lap, afraid he would see them trembling. 'I go the same dressmaker as Tassy, you know.'

'You couldn't do better,' he said heartily. 'She's an elegant girl, though not a patch on you.'

He placed his hand on Sharon's arm and she restrained a shiver. Although he was acting normally there was a flush on his cheeks and a tenseness in his bearing that could either imply excitement at his victory or guilt at how he had achieved it.

'Thanks for the compliment, Pete, but you can't compare us. Tassy's a high flier under her smooth manner.'

'Oh really? I don't quite follow you.'

'I mean she's not just a pretty face.'

'Neither are you.'

'But I'm not a girl with influence—like Tassy. She has an important father and she takes advantage of it.'

'True,' Pete conceded. 'She likes exercising power.'

'Was she there when her father announced the winner of the contract?'

'Yes.'

'Was she pleased?'

'I didn't ask.'

'I'm sure she was, though,' Sharon persisted. 'After all, she knows you quite well.'

'Not as well as she knows Kane,' Pete grinned. 'So you've no reason to be jealous. Though I'd like it if you were.'

'Sorry to disappoint you,' Sharon drawled, delighted her next remark could be the most truthful she had ever uttered to him. 'Any feelings I had for you died months ago.'

'Oh.' He was disconcerted. 'I was hoping I still meant something to you.'

'Which proves how little you know me.' She took a deep breath, then said deliberately: 'I saw Tassy leave Kane's suite at two o'clock this morning.'

In the act of raising his glass, Pete stopped. 'Miaow, miaow, sweetheart. Don't you know it's not nice to tittle tattle? Anyway, who cares what she does?'

'I thought *you* might.'

'You've got to be kidding? Tassy means nothing to me.'

'In that case, perhaps you can give me some advice.'

'About what?'

'About what I should do. You see I found one of my hotel master keys in the pocket of the dress she was wearing the night she and Kane had dinner with us.'

Pete stared at Sharon blankly, and for a long moment seemed incapable of speech. But when he finally found his voice it was faintly amused. 'Don't tell me you've become a pickpocket! How did *you* find it?'

'I didn't. It was Lala—the dressmaker.' Crisply Sharon recounted the story, watching carefully as she did. But neither by word nor expression did he show any concern.

'You probably dropped it from your bag and Tassy found it,' he said nonchalantly. 'She couldn't have known who it belonged to.'

Sharon knew perfectly well the master key had been on the ring with the others, but did not say so, since she wasn't sure if he was covering up for Tassy or genuinely believed what he was saying.

Abruptly he stood up. 'Come on,' he said, 'let's take a stroll. Your imagination's working overtime.'

With some reluctance she followed him outside, reassuring herself he could hardly do her any harm if she stayed within sight and sound of the hotel.

The night was warm and clear, with the Milky Way rseplendent in the sky, and the cicadas persistent in their chorus. Sharon looked up at the hotel but saw no light in Kane's suite. Damn! She had not told Reception where she would be.

'I can't stay out here long, Pete. I've still some work to do.'

'At this time of night? You're crazy. With your looks you could be a model and earn ten times what you get from the Avonmore.'

'I'd hate the work though. Being happy in my job is far more important to me.'

'I couldn't be happy in a job unless I felt it was paying me what I was worth,' Pete said.

'One's own worth may be different from the price other people put on it,' Sharon replied, looking him full in the face.

'Then I'd find a job with people who thought the same as I did!'

'Like the Japanese company?'

'Right. They're a great outfit, Sharon.' He moved closer and put his arm around her waist. 'But let's talk about us instead. I know what you said inside just now, but if we——'

'No Pete,' she interrupted, 'I'm tired of play acting. It's a year too late. You know it as well as I do.'

'No, I don't. I was a fool last year, sweetheart, and I——'

'Stop it Pete. It's no use.' She moved away from him. 'I must get back.'

As calmly as she could she walked towards the hotel,

skirting the poolside, where late-night diners were still at their tables, and threading her way through the outdoor bar. But once inside, she ran through the main reception rooms again, in search of Kane, then went to talk to Johnny, the night clerk.

'Any sign of Mr Morgan yet?'

'You've just missed him,' came the answer. 'Didn't he call you? I told him you wanted to speak to him urgently.'

Sharon shook her head, fighting back the tears. 'Did he say what time he'll be back?'

'He won't be back. He's on his way to England!'

She was aghast. 'But—but he can't be! There's no plane at this hour.'

'Yes there is,' Johnny said. 'The eight o'clock from Hong Kong came in late, and won't be leaving Bangkok until one. Mr Morgan managed to get a seat on it.'

'Why didn't you let me know?'

'I didn't think it necessary. I'm very sorry, Miss Kingston. I gave him your message and I thought he——'

'I understand,' she said quickly, not wishing to upset him, and castigated herself for not being more precise. Yet she had never anticipated Kane leaving tonight. This was terrible. She simply had to speak to him tell him what she had discovered and hope it would clear her name. She looked at her watch. If she moved fast she could catch Kane before he boarded his flight.

'Would you order me a car, Johnny? I've got to talk to Mr Morgan before he leaves.'

'I'll take you, if you like,' the young man volunteered. 'I love driving and I can get Kim to stand in for me here. I'm sure I can borrow one of the hotel cars.'

Delighted by the offer, Sharon accepted, and within minutes they were speeding towards the capital. She was too tense to make small talk; not that Johnny appeared to mind. He handled the Chevrolet with the precision of a first-class rally driver, and the car ate up the miles. They reached the airport with half-an-hour to spare, and Sharon threw a 'thank you' at the young clerk, before dashing into the Departure Hall.

To her dismay the London-bound passengers had already gone through Immigration, and her heart sank. The Thais, though unfailingly polite, made heavy weather of rules, and she doubted her chances of getting through to speak to Kane. None the less she intended having a darn good try. Fortuitously she had her passport with her, as well as her work permit from the Avonmore, which showed her position with them, and boldly she approached Passport Control and explained it was imperative she see Mr Morgan.

'Mr Bonlam left a message at our hotel for him,' she lied boldly, 'and I have to give it to him personally.'

The official frowned. 'Is not possible. No one permitted go through here unless they leave country.'

'But I *have* to see Mr Morgan. You can check with the Ministry if you like,' she added, crossing her fingers.

Still the man hesitated, and Sharon looked him firmly in the eye. 'Call Mr Bonlam himself, if you don't believe me. I'd rather he lost his temper with you than *me*.'

The man glanced at the wall clock. 'Very well, then. But you no stay long.'

Sharon could have kissed him; instead she raced past the barrier to the Departure Lounge. Even at this hour it was half-full, and she looked anxiously about her. It wasn't easy to spot anyone in the teeming mass and she had very little time. Heart beating madly, she pushed her way through the crowd, then magically saw a tall, lean figure with gleaming dark hair.

'Kane!' she called above the hubbub. 'Kane!'

He heard her and turned, his expression forbidding. But nothing could put her off, and she ran over to him and clutched his arm.

'Thank heavens I've found you,' she gasped. 'I've got to explain about the key and where it was. I never touched your papers, Kane. I swear it. It was Tassy.'

'Don't give me that!' Angrily he tried to dislodge her hand. 'Trust you to blame somebody else. Don't think——'

'You're the one who isn't thinking!' Sharon stormed. 'I tell you it was Tassy!'

'I don't——'

'Listen to me, will you?' Sharon almost screamed the words, too overwrought to care what anyone around them might think. Then not giving him a chance to interrupt her, she poured out the story of the key and where it had been found.

'If you think I'm lying, ring Lala and ask her. Tassy's one of her best customers and she wouldn't make up a story to help me. Ask her, I tell you!'

'I don't need to. Tassy couldn't have seen my papers. I've always kept them in my safe, and I never left my suite unless I locked them back up.'

'But last night she——'

'I didn't take them from the safe until after I'd seen her home,' Kane interrupted.

Sharon marvelled that even at a time like this, he should still pretend he and Tassy weren't lovers. 'Then you must be the original Invisible Man!'

'What's that supposed to mean?'

'That I didn't see you with her when she left your room at two o'clock this morning!'

'This morning?' he echoed.

'Don't play the innocent, Kane. I don't give a damn what you do in your private life—or your public one, come to that—so long as you don't brand *me* a thief! I saw Tassy leaving your suite at two o'clock this morning. She didn't take the elevator, and went down the back stairs.'

'Tassy wasn't in my suite last night,' Kane bit out. 'I saw her home, as I said, and came straight back to go through my papers and get them ready for today's meeting. Then I went to sleep.'

'If that's the truth, perhaps you should work out what your girlfriend was doing in your suite while you were in dreamland,' Sharon retorted. 'You're intelligent enough! You should——'

The rest of Sharon's words were drowned by a voice over the Tannoy ordering all passengers for the flight to London to board the aircraft, and she stared at Kane, silently willing him to ignore it.

'Before you go, I've one question to ask you,' he said abruptly. 'What were *you* doing prowling round my floor at 2 a.m.?'

'I had a right to be there,' she snapped. 'You aren't the only guest on that floor, you know. I had to settle in some late arrivals.'

Sickened by his accusatory tone, and without waiting for his reply, she swung round and ran out. She had done all she could to clear her name, and if he did not believe her, then so be it.

During the return drive to Pattaya, Sharon found it impossible to stop thinking of Tassy's behaviour. As far as the girl was concerned she would not want to be implicated in any theft of documents, and must have intended returning the master key to Sharon's bag. But how? Pete seemed the most feasible answer. Tassy must have planned to give him the key once she had finished with it, and leave it to him to put it in Sharon's room later that night when she was asleep.

Except that Tassy had lost it. Or thought she had! Thank goodness Lala was such a meticulous dressmaker! Had she not been the key would have fallen on the carpet somewhere, and no one would have known how it had got there. But what had Tassy thought when she had discovered she had lost the key—not realising it was in the hem of her dress all the time? Whatever her panic, she had obviously decided to play it cool. After all, a lost key could never be traced to her. And never would have been, had not Lala found it.

Through the windscreen, Sharon saw the winking red light of an aircraft as it began to climb.

'The plane to London,' Johnny said. 'I wish I was on it.'

'So do I,' she echoed, and thought again of Kane, and what he might do.

If he believed her story, he would need a statement from Lala, corroborating it. If the woman refused to give it—which she might, since Tassy was not only a member of an important family, but an excellent client of hers—then Sharon's story could never be substantiated, and Kane would have no chance of making Mr Bonlam reconsider his decision about the contract. On the other hand Kane might well decide to let sleeping dogs lie. His company was not short of work so why bother raking up the dirt and possibly cause a political storm that could make it impossible for him to get any other contracts in Thailand?

'You still upset, Miss Kingston?' Johnny asked.

'No,' she replied. 'What makes you think I am?'

'You keep sighing.'

'I'm tired. It's been a long day.'

'But you saw Mr Morgan and everything was all right?'

'I did what I had to do,' she said slowly. 'But I'm not sure how right things are.'

'I don't like to see you sad,' Johnny murmured. 'A lovely woman should always be smiling.'

'Watch me tomorrow and I'll try to oblige,' she said with enforced gaiety, then leaned back and closed her eyes, pretending to rest.

But her mind was racing, fast as the jet taking Kane half-way across the world. Yet what did it matter how far he was from her, when they were already worlds apart?

CHAPTER FIFTEEN

THE days dragged endlessely, and Sharon ate, worked and slept as in a dream. Try though she did not to think of Kane, it was impossible, and the sound of a man's deep voice or the turn of a dark head brought him instantly to mind.

She still found it incredible that after all she had said to him at the airport he had persisted in leaving for London. He should at least have checked her story and not dismissed it out of hand!

The weekend after his departure there was an influx of tourists, filling the gap left by the delegates. In a matter of weeks it would be the monsoon season, when all but the most intrepid visitors would depart. Once this happened she would return to Bangkok, but wherever she was, memories of Kane, and his cruel impugning of her character, would haunt her waking hours and give nightmares to her sleeping ones.

She did not see Lala until she went to collect her pink dress the following Wednesday, and with careful casualness asked about Tassy.

'I haven't seen her,' the dressmaker replied. 'Her maid called in to collect the brocade dress and said Miss Bonlam was going to Tokyo.'

'To Tokyo?' Sharon was incredulous.

'For a vacation,' Lala explained. 'Miss Bonlam has some friends there I believe.'

And one friend in particular, Sharon thought grimly, and no longer had a shadow of a doubt that Tassy and Pete had been in league together. She wondered if Kane knew where Tassy had gone, yet even as the thought came to mind, she realised it was impossible, for he was thousands of miles away. Even if he kept in touch with Tassy, she was unlikely to have told him she was off to see the man who had won the contract away from him!

For the hundredth time Sharon puzzled over the Thai girl's behaviour. Had the Japanese company paid her to steal for them, or was infatuation for Pete the reason? Remembering his easy charm and how she herself had fallen for it, she was inclined to think the latter. Yet how cleverly the two of them had played their cards; pretending they were casual acquaintances, with Pete maintaining he was still interested in herself, while Tassy had strung Kane along.

Sharon sighed, accepting the fact that when the dust settled, she would be the only one left to nurse a lasting hurt. Kane would win other contracts and the loss of this one would be forgotten; Tassy's affair with Pete would either blossom—in which case they deserved each other—or would peter out when passion died, and they went their own selfish ways. It was a depressing admission, and by the time she returned to the hotel she was ready to howl with rage and despair.

Instead, she changed into one of her new cottons and went for a stroll along the beach.

The sand was still warm and she took off her sandals and dangled them from her hand as she allowed the sea to lap against her toes, then stopped to watch the lacy foam made by the waves as they broke on the shore.

As always happened in the tropics, dusk fell swiftly, and by the time she returned to the road, the azure sky was tinged with red and the coral islands fast fading into the gloom. She had walked further than she had intended and was a good mile from the hotel.

Several taxis plied for hire, and one driver followed

her, refusing to give up. Knowing that to smile would encourage him, Sharon shook her head angrily and quickened her pace. It reminded her she had met Kane in similar circumstances, when he had rescued her on the busy streets of Bangkok. How cockily assured she had been on the surface, and how glad of his commanding presence to rescue her.

But Kane was a world away, and always would be, and she had only herself to rely on. Furiously she rounded on the taxi driver, her expression making it clear she had reached the end of her tether, and he gave her a cheeky grin and accelerated away.

In the hotel again, she noticed a pile of papers lying on the Reception Desk. They were copies of the Avonmore's own news sheet, which gave details of activities at the Bangkok and Pattaya hotels, and listed all prominent visitors, both present and those to come.

Idly she took one to her room, poured herself a fruit juice and settled down to read until dinner time. She flicked through the pages, interested in seeing the different activities laid on by the city hotel. At Pattaya, guests were left far more to their own devices, and she had a sneaking suspicion many would prefer to have their days organised, finding it boring to lie too long in the sun. She would have a word with Bud Cameron and see if they could lay on some outings. There were day trips to the Coral Islands, of course, but an evening barbecue there would be exciting and romantic.

She turned to the centre page stopping abruptly as she found herself staring at Kane.

So he was back in Bangkok! Had been there three days, according to the newsletter. To know he was in the country and had not bothered contacting her, confirmed everything she had thought earlier this evening, and in an agony of bitterness she flung herself on the bed and cried as though her heart would break.

The ringing of the telephone brought her upright, and stemming her tears, she lifted the receiver. It was Johnny, unusually agitated.

'Sorry to bother you, Miss Kingston, but one of the guests is making a fuss about his suite and wants to move to the penthouse floor. We have nothing vacant there for two days, and if you could placate him . . . It's 507.'

'Can't I see him tomorrow?' Sharon asked, touching her tear-swollen face, and knowing what a sight she must look. 'I'm off duty, and I didn't plan on coming down tonight.'

'I realise that,' Johnny said swiftly. 'But he's in a terrible temper. If you could just see him and explain that we hope to move him tomorrow . . .'

'All right,' she sighed. 'I'll go see what I can do. But I'm in no mood to placate anyone tonight.'

'You'll still manage to do so.' There was a smile in Johnny's voice. 'You could charm a piranha, Miss Kingston.'

'I'll tell him that,' she said dryly. 'I'll be on my way in five minutes.'

It was nearly fifteen before she was. Her eyes had required several applications of iced water to bring them back to normal. Well, not quite normal, for the lids remained puffy and she had been forced to apply lavish eyeshadow and mascara. Deciding that though she felt like death, there was no reason to look it, she deliberately put on her new pink silk. It was too expensive to leave hanging in the wardrobe, and she was suddenly determined that from now on she would not allow thoughts of Kane determine her actions.

Suite 507 was at the back of the hotel, and did not have a view of the sea, and she was not surprised the guest was complaining. She rang the buzzer, and hardly had her hand dropped to her side when the door was flung violently open and she found herself staring at a tall, lean man, black hair gleaming, bright eyes watchful.

Kane Morgan!

Sharon thought she was going to faint. The blood seemed to seep from her head and she swayed and clutched at the wall. Firm hands came out to steady her, then drew her forward, close against him.

'Sorry I gave you such a shock,' he said huskily, his breath stirring her hair. 'But I made the clerk at Reception swear he wouldn't give my identity away. I wanted to surprise you.'

'You've certainly done that.' Amazingly she was able to keep her voice steady as she pushed him away and stepped out of his hold. 'I was told you were unhappy with your suite and——'

'Not any more,' he interposed. 'Not now *you're* here. Come inside, Sharon. We have to talk.'

'More accusations?' she asked sarcastically.

'Only against myself. I've been a blind fool and . . .' He put out his hand to touch her, but seeing the look on her face, did not do so. 'Just give me five minutes of your time,' he pleaded.

She hesitated, then stepped through the door. At once she saw a bottle of champagne in an ice bucket, and two glasses.

'A celebration,' he murmured, seeing her glance at the table.

'To celebrate what?'

'My getting the contract.'

Too astounded to speak, she sank down on the nearest chair.

'Pete Wilburg's firm have withdrawn,' Kane went on. 'A lot of things have happened since I last saw you.' He seemed about to say more, then unexpectedly went over to stand by the window.

His dark head was framed by the partially drawn wine-red curtains, and Sharon was reminded of a Spanish grandee in a portrait by Goya. A tired grandee though, if the deep lines either side of his mouth were anything to go by. She clenched her hands and stifled the urge to hold them out to him.

'I read in the Avonmore Newsletter you were back in Bangkok,' she said instead.

'I've been there a few days but I deliberately didn't call you.' He seemed unabashed to admit it.

'I didn't expect you to,' she said.

'I hope you don't mean that?'

She remained silent and he took a step towards her, then stopped. 'No, I daren't come close. I've things to say first, and until I have ...' His shoulders straightened, and he looked like a man preparing for battle. 'I didn't ignore what you told me at the airport, Sharon, though you obviously thought I did. But I was so staggered by what you'd said, I couldn't take it in.'

'You mean you couldn't believe me!'

'Well ... It was a very far-fetched story,' he said in self-defence.

'You mean it wasn't far-fetched to think *me* a thief?' she accused, her anger against him rising again.

'No—yes! Oh for heaven's sake, Sharon, try to see it from my point of view. What you said at the airport bowled me over, but by the time I touched down in London, I was thinking clearly again. I began to have a few ideas of my own, and I immediately started making enquiries about Pete's activities when he'd been living in England. I wanted to ascertain who he'd seen, who his friends were.'

'Me, of course,' Sharon said. 'His accomplice in crime!'

Kane half-smiled. 'You know I don't think that any more, so stop being perverse and feminine!'

'You——'

'Shut up and let me finish,' he cut across her. 'If you don't, I'll . . .'

With a visible effort he controlled himself, and looking at him, Sharon knew he was at the end of his tether. To go on being antagonistic towards him was childish, though if he thought she was going to fall into his arms like a ripe plum, he had another think coming.

'I'm listening,' she said quietly.

'Thank God for that!' He raked his fingers through his hair, and a dark lock fell forward. 'As I was saying—or trying to say, my enquiries about Wilburg yielded some very interesting information.' He paused. 'When he lived in London, he was seeing Tassy there!'

'Tassy!'

'Yes. It seems she came to England every three months for a week or ten days, and they were inseparable.'

Sharon thought back, remembering the many occasions Pete had not contacted her, pleading business commitments. So even then, he had been two-timing her! It was a salutary thought.

'The moment I realised they knew each other so well,' Kane was still speaking, 'everything fell into place. I knew then that I'd made a dreadful mistake about you. You were right about everything, Sharon. Tassy stole your key and photographed my plans. I have no proof, so it's only conjecture, but I'm a hundred per cent positive that's what happened.'

'But without proof, what could you do? I mean, how did you manage to get the contract away from him?'

'I called Bonlam from London and told him I was

returning to Thailand to see him. When I did, I told him everything that *you'd* told me, and while he was still protesting that it was impossible, I gave him a dossier on his daughter's meetings with Pete in London and New York.'

'They met in New York as well?' Sharon was startled.

'Oh yes. It's where they *first* met, as it so happens. I knew she'd done her business studies there, so I contacted a top detective agency to dig up everything they could about her. It cost a fortune, but it was worth a hundred times what I paid! They found old roommates of hers who knew all about her affair with Pete. One of them even had snaps of them taken in Sun Valley on a skiing weekend! My man flew to the hotel and got a copy of the Register showing they'd stayed there as Mr and Mrs Wilburg. That clinched it for Bonlam. And for good measure I said you and Lala would testify that the master key was found in Tassy's pocket, and you'd also seen her coming out of my room at 2 a.m. the night before the meeting.'

'Lala would never have testified to anything,' Sharon said, still not able to absorb all she had heard.

'I knew that,' Kane said. 'But Bonlam didn't. All *he* knew was that he was up a gum tree and in a very sticky position! He was scared to tell the Prime Minister what Tassy had done, so he called her in Tokyo—her being there, by the way, reinforced everything I'd said—and he insisted she make Pete's company give up the contract. If they didn't, he told her I'd create a scandal that would force him to resign and might even lead to criminal charges against her.'

'You wouldn't——'

'Of course not. But Bonlam didn't know that. As far as he was concerned, I was ready to bring down the Government!'

'I can't take it all in.' Sharon drew a steadying breath. 'Are you saying she and Pete just caved in without putting up a fight? There must be more to it than that.'

'Why? They were scared that I meant to carry out my threats. And if Bonlam and Tassy were disgraced, the Thai government would have to do the honourable thing and re-open all the negotiations, which would mean the entire project being set back for another year. But if Wilburg simply pulled out, then my tender would then be the next best, as it was genuinely the lowest.'

'So all's well that ends well,' Sharon murmured.

'Businesswise, yes,' Kane said. 'But in personal terms, I'm not thinking of an end. Only a beginning. *Our* beginning.'

Sharon turned her head away, unwilling for him to see the pain in her eyes. His lack of trust still hurt deeply and she could not forget it as easily as he imagined. Besides, they had no future together, for she had no intention of being his girlfriend.

'I know you cared for Pete at one time,' he went on quietly. 'But how did you feel when you saw him again here?'

'I've already answered that question. Why should I repeat it?'

'Because I want confirmation. I can't live without you, Sharon, and I have to be sure you no longer give a damn about anyone else! When I flew back here last time and found you in his arms, I was so furious I could have strangled you.'

'Well I've no intention of dropping into *your* arms,' she retorted. 'So go find someone else to play with.'

'No!' In two strides he was beside her, hauling her up from the chair. 'It's you or no one. I've never felt like this about any woman. When I left you that first time in Bangkok, I was positive I'd get over you. You were a beautiful girl and I wanted you, but when you said no, I told myself I'd soon find someone else. But I didn't—couldn't—even though I tried. After you, no woman meant anything to me. All I could think of was your sweetness, your humour, your warmth.'

'And also that I'd refused to be another scalp in your collection,' she taunted, reluctant to believe he meant anything beyond that. 'I'm sure you found solace with Tassy.'

'Not after I met you.' Kane's hands dropped away from her and once again he stepped back. His body was rigid and there was undeniable tension in the set of his mouth. 'I haven't touched a woman since the first night I went out with you. To begin with I couldn't figure out why—thought I was getting old! But as soon as I was back in England I knew the real reason. I'd fallen in love with you.' He paused, as if waiting for her to speak, and when she didn't, he frowned. 'Do you find it so hard to believe me, Sharon? I know I've played around, but so have most unattached men. But once you came into my life, every other woman faded away. It took me a while to work out why, and to accept it, but once I did, I knew I'd settle for nothing less than having you on a permanent basis.'

'Permanent?' Sharon echoed.

'Yes. I want to marry you and look after you. Spend the rest of my life making you happy!'

Sharon swallowed hard. Kane wanted to marry her. It was a word she had never expected to hear him say, and it was as hard for her to take in as the earlier part of his story.

'I realise that the way I acted towards you—the things I said—must have hurt you pretty badly,' he went on jerkily, 'and my only excuse is that I was so jealous I couldn't think straight.'

'You're not thinking straight now,' she said sweetly, still reluctant to fall into his arms. 'You accuse me of playing fast and loose when it suits me, and then to top it all you believe I stole your plans and gave them to a rival! If I was that sort of girl, you really *would* deserve me! But since I'm not, you'd better start looking for someone who is!'

'It's you or no one.'

'I'm sure you'll change your mind. You're not cut out to be a monk!'

'You can say that again!' His eyes glittered and he moved closer to her. 'Hate me as much as you like, Sharon, I deserve it. But I'm still going to lay siege to you.' His arms came out to engulf her. 'Starting now!'

He lowered his head swiftly and covered her mouth with his. Stubbornly she kept her lips shut, but he refused to be put off, and his mouth continued to move upon hers. Yet he did not try to force it open, relying instead on the play of his hands on her body.

And how skilful they were! Ranging across her back and down her spine to press her close to his thighs, where she could feel the surge and thrust of his need for her; caressing the smooth skin of her shoulders and then skilfully unzipping the pink silk bodice to cup her full, firm breasts.

She struggled to free herself as his fingers touched her nipples, but his grip tightened and he pushed her down on to the settee and covered her with his body. He was murmuring in his throat, words of love and passion she had thought never to hear from him.

'My dearest . . . my heart . . . mother of my children . . . only you . . . only you.'

Then he was stroking her again, sending sharp spasms of desire through her body, which she could not control. But why should she? This was Kane, the man she loved and wanted above all others. He had paid the price for doubting her—she had seen it in the new lines on his face—and to make him go on paying would cost her dear, too. Twining her arms around his neck, she parted her lips. For an instant he did not seem sure she was surrendering, then with a deep-throated murmur, his tongue penetrated the moist sweetness of her mouth.

Passion rose between them with an intensity that brooked no shyness, no simulation. Clothes were discarded and skin lay upon skin as they clung to one another with unashamed abandon. Many times Sharon had imagined this moment of surrender, but never had she envisaged it as tempestuous as this, as frenzied, sensual, heart-stopping.

Kane was passionate and demanding, yet tender too, aware of her innocence and, initially, careful not to shock. But soon he sensed that her love for him was all-encompassing, and that whatever he did, she wanted and revelled in, intent only on absorbing him into her, having him explore and touch every swell and curve and hidden cleft, rousing her to such mindless ecstasy that when his malehood thrust deep into her body, she was moist and ready for him, thighs parted to receive him as he exploded within her, flooding her with life-giving sperm and making her wholly and completely his.

For aeons they seemed to float, suspended in a drowsy sea of satiated desire. But eventually they returned to reality, and he lifted himself slightly away from her, the better to look into her eyes.

'When will you marry me?' he demanded. 'I won't know any peace till you're mine.'

Mine. The word jolted her sanguinity, and the rosy future took on a bleaker hue.

'I'm *mine*, Kane,' she said flatly. 'I'm a person with her own thoughts, her own wishes and needs. Don't regard me as a possession.'

'I'm sorry,' he said swiftly. 'I didn't mean it the way it sounded. I just want to tell the world we belong to each other. That I'm as much yours as I want you to be mine. But you can still lead your own life.'

'I can?' She half-sat up and felt his eyes rivet themselves on the swollen roundness of her breasts.

'You can,' he agreed thickly. 'I know what your career means to you, and I don't expect you to give it up. All I ask is that you let me share your life.'

'Even if I'm given a hotel in Devon or Skye to manage, or one abroad perhaps?'

'Wherever,' he said. 'From now on I'm letting Mark and a few others of my men do most of our overseas work. Any future travelling I do, will be only to spend time with *you*.'

She could not believe he meant it, but the gravity of his expression told her he did, and she marvelled that love could have such an effect on him. Yet why not? Look at the effect it was having on her! The realisation of exactly how much, was only slowly being borne in on her, and she lay silent, absorbing and understanding what it was doing to her entire outlook.

'You'll hate my career, Kane. You say you won't, but I honestly can't see you enjoying sharing me with my job. It's a full-time one, you know.'

'Only too well! But I've given it a lot of thought, Sharon, and I find that sharing you is a darn sight better than not having you. I'll do anything to stay in your life.'

'Even coming second to my career?'

'Even that,' he said ruefully. 'You see, I have no choice.'

'But *I* have. Loving each other won't be enough. Oh

we'll work things out in the beginning—for the first year perhaps—but after that? Well, I'm not so sure. My having a career wouldn't fit in with your life.'

'I'll change my life to suit yours,' he assured her swiftly. 'I'm not making idle promises, Sharon. I mean them.'

'I know you do. But I tell you it wouldn't work. You'd start out with all sorts of good intentions, but eventually some crisis would blow up somewhere in the world where your company's working, and you'd have to fly there and stay there for weeks on end; maybe months.'

'No,' he affirmed. 'I'd send Mark or someone else. And even if I did have to go, it would only be for a fleeting visit.'

'Oh darling,' she laughed. 'You mean what you're saying now, but you'd change your mind if you really had a major crisis on your hands. And if it *was* major, then I'd want to be with you, sharing your worries.'

He pulled back, the better to look into her face. 'What exactly are you trying to tell me, Sharon?'

'Don't you know?'

'I'm not sure.'

'You mean you think you know but you're scared of saying it out loud in case you're wrong! And of course you're also worried in case I think you're trying to pressurise me.'

His rueful expression told her she was right, and she smiled. Seeing the corners of her mouth turn up, Kane lowered his head and touched his lips to hers.

'The one problem in falling in love with a clever woman,' he opined, 'is that she can sometimes be too clever! All right, so the occasional crisis will blow up, but being with you—our marriage—will always take priority. You've got to believe that, Sharon.'

'I do. Because our marriage will take priority with

me too. That's why I know I have to give up the Avonmore.'

'But——'

'No buts, Kane. You know what you're capable of, and *I* know what I can do. And the one thing I can't, is cope with you and a hotel and six children.'

'*What?*'

'Well, maybe five. But definitely four! You've so much to give a family, darling.' Her voice shook and she pressed her cheek to his. 'You're not only a brilliant engineer and marvellous businessman, but a generous human being who has the courage to admit when he's wrong.'

'Hey,' he protested huskily. 'Don't make me out to be better than I am.'

'Better or best?' she teased. 'I don't know you well enough yet to be sure!'

'You asking for more?'

'Certainly not.'

'Pity,' he whispered upon her mouth. 'I was hoping you would say yes.'

'Maybe I will, with a bit of encouragement.'

Promptly he began kissing her, his lips gentle, his hands tender in their exploration as he roused her to trembling passion.

Her hands reached for him, caressing his hair and the firm back, sliding her fingers along his spine and down his thighs.

'You know what this will lead to, don't you?' he growled.

'Yes. Does that make me insatiable?'

'No!' His teeth nipped her tongue lightly. 'It makes you wonderful, adorable.'

His voice deepened, grew more urgent, and fiercely he parted her legs and thrust into her again. Though she had not anticipated his swift arousal, she was ready for him, and this second time she was not inhibited by shyness. After all, this was Kane, the man she loved with all her being, the man soon to be her husband. With a glad cry she responded, moving her body in time with his until they were both soaring high, unconscious of time or place, knowing only each other's needs and intent on fulfilling them.

'I want you!' he cried. 'Oh Sharon, I can't hold back.'

'Don't,' she breathed into his mouth. 'I want you too. So much, Kane, so much!'

In a soaring climax he flooded her with his love. She screamed in ecstasy and her fingers raked across his back as she shuddered to her own climax, knowing that her awakened womanhood would only bring her joy as long as this man was in her life.

He gently lifted himself away from her and lay beside her, and only then did she notice they were no longer on the settee, but lying upon the rug in front of the terrace window.

As if aware she had just realised it, he grinned.

'I kept you on the floor on purpose,' he admitted, 'because I didn't want you telling your parents I'd taken you to bed before marrying you!'

She burst out laughing, and as he saw the creamy swell of her throat, he pressed his lips to it.

'The British Consul here is a friend of mine,' he went on, 'and I'm sure he can expedite a licence. Will the end of the week suit you?'

'So soon?' she gasped. 'My parents——'

'I'll fly them over. No problem. But if you'd rather wait to marry in England, we'll fly back as soon as I've negotiated my contract with Bonlam. But that won't be for about three weeks.'

'By which time my back will be stuck to this rug!' she giggled. 'No way, Kane. I'll talk to Mum and Da and insist they fly out. I'm sure they'll be delighted. You're a great catch for a working girl!'

He growled in mock anger and pulled her over until she was on top of him.

'Kane, don't,' she protested. 'What about the champagne you promised me?'

'It will be great after.'

She felt his body stir again, the movement exciting her to her own arousal. 'After what?' she asked huskily.

'I'll give you three guesses,' he said.

'I only need one.'

'And I only need you,' he murmured into her mouth. 'Only you.'

Here's how to get this special offer from Harlequin!

As simple as 1...2...3!

1. Each month, save one Treasury Edition coupon from your favorite Romance or Presents novel.
2. In four months you'll have saved four Treasury Edition coupons (<u>only one coupon</u> per month allowed).
3. Then all you have to do is fill out and return the order form provided, along with the four Treasury Edition coupons required and $1.00 for postage and handling.

Mail to: Harlequin Reader Service

RT1-B-2

In the U.S.A.
2504 West Southern Ave.
Tempe, AZ 85282

In Canada
P.O. Box 2800, Postal Station A
5170 Yonge Street
Willowdale, Ont. M2N 6J3

Please send me my FREE copy of the Janet Dailey Treasury Edition. I have enclosed the four Treasury Edition coupons required and $1.00 for postage and handling along with this order form.

(Please Print)

NAME_____

ADDRESS_____

CITY_____

STATE/PROV._____ ZIP/POSTAL CODE_____

SIGNATURE_____
This offer is limited to one order per household.

SUPPLIES LIMITED

This special Janet Dailey offer expires January 1986.

H·A·R·L·E·Q·U·I·N

FIRST·CLASS
Sweepstakes

OFFICIAL RULES

1. NO PURCHASE NECESSARY. To enter, complete the official entry/order form. Be sure to indicate whether or not you wish to take advantage of our subscription offer.

2. Entry blanks have been preselected for the prizes offered. Your response will be checked to see if you are a winner. In the event that these preselected responses are not claimed, a random drawing will be held from all entries received to award not less than $150,000 in prizes. This is in addition to any free, surprise or mystery gifts which might be offered. Versions of this sweepstakes with different prizes will appear in Preview Service Mailings by Harlequin Books and their affiliates. Winners selected will receive the prize offered in their sweepstakes brochure.

3. This promotion is being conducted under the supervision of Marden-Kane, an independent judging organization. By entering the sweepstakes, each entrant accepts and agrees to be bound by these rules and the decisions of the judges, which shall be final and binding. Odds of winning in the random drawing are dependent upon the total number of entries received. Taxes, if any, are the sole responsibility of the prize winners. Prizes are nontransferable. All entries must be received by August 31, 1986.

4. The following prizes will be awarded:

      (1) Grand Prize: Rolls-Royce™ or $100,000 Cash!
      (Rolls-Royce being offered by permission of
      Rolls-Royce Motors Inc.)

      (1) Second Prize: A trip for two to Paris for 7 days/6 nights. Trip includes air transportation on the Concorde, hotel accommodations...PLUS...$5,000 spending money!

      (1) Third Prize: A luxurious Mink Coat!

5. This offer is open to residents of the U.S. and Canada, 18 years or older, except employees of Harlequin Books, its affiliates, subsidiaries, Marden-Kane and all other agencies and persons connected with conducting this sweepstakes. All Federal, State and local laws apply. Void in the province of Quebec and wherever prohibited or restricted by law. Winners will be notified by mail and may be required to execute an affidavit of eligibility and release, which must be returned within 14 days after notification. Canadian winners will be required to answer a skill-testing question. Winners consent to the use of their name, photograph and/or likeness for advertising and publicity purposes in conjunction with this and similar promotions without additional compensation. One prize per family or household.

6. For a list of our most current prize winners, send a stamped, self-addressed envelope to: WINNERS LIST, c/o Marden-Kane, P.O. Box 10404, Long Island City, New York 11101

You're invited to accept 4 books and a surprise gift Free!

Acceptance Card

Mail to: Harlequin Reader Service®

In the U.S.
2504 West Southern Ave.
Tempe, AZ 85282

In Canada
P.O. Box 2800, Postal Station A
5170 Yonge Street
Willowdale, Ontario M2N 6J3

YES! Please send me 4 free Harlequin Presents® novels and my free surprise gift. Then send me 8 brand new novels every month as they come off the presses. Bill me at the low price of $1.75 each ($1.95 in Canada) — an 11% saving off the retail price. There are no shipping, handling or other hidden costs. There is no minimum number of books I must purchase. I can always return a shipment and cancel at any time. Even if I never buy another book from Harlequin, the 4 free novels and the surprise gift are mine to keep forever.

108 BPP-BPGE

Name _____ (PLEASE PRINT)

Address _____ Apt. No. _____

City _____ State/Prov. _____ Zip/Postal Code _____

This offer is limited to one order per household and not valid to present subscribers. Price is subject to change.

ACP-SUB-1